Revenge via Death

"Come on Marcus!" called out the procurator.

"Come on the traitor's son!" called someone else. It was a cry that Marcus had not heard for many months.

"The whelp's the coward that his traitor father was!" It was said loud enough for every man there to hear.

It was easy for him to skip under the swinging metal balls being thrust at him, as he watched for the men with the poles. He was fending them off with the small buckler on his left arm, and cutting occasionally with the sword in his right. The huge open courtyard rang to a shrill scream. Every head turned. Then he saw the Thracian, his face seeming frozen with concentration and hatred—lunging at him with his blunted spear.

Only it wasn't blunted! The point flicked at him like the tongue of a snake ready to attack. Time froze, and Marcus knew he was going to die. He was the victim of one of his father's murderers. His last thoughts were of anger and frustration . . .

NORTH COMPLEX

The Gladiator Series:

The Gladiator...
Blood on the Sand
by Andrew Quiller

PINNACLE BOOKS   LOS ANGELES

GLADIATOR #4: BLOOD ON THE SAND

A Pinnacle Books edition, published by special arrangement with Granada Publishing Ltd., London

ISBN: 0-523-40094-2

First printing, January 1978

Cover illustration by Ken Kelly

Printed in the United States of America

PINNACLE BOOKS, INC.
One Century Plaza
2029 Century Park East
Los Angeles, California 90067

This is for Bill Antrobus, who deceived me for many years into believing that the E.M.F. of a Leclanché cell was 1.1 when it is, of course, about 1.5 volts. Despite that he's still a friend, and I hope that things go well out west for him and for Michelle, Steven and Robert.

BLOOD ON THE SAND

ONE

The stench of sun-baked blood caught you by the nostrils. Mingled with the sweat of nearly fifty thousand men and women. Freeborn and slaves. Packing the ranks of seats in the massive Flavian Amphitheater upward and upward, until they merged and vanished in the pit of shadow beneath the striped awning of canvas. The velarium, hauled creakingly to its place on a web of ropes and pulleys, giving the illusion of coolness to the excited mob.

Far out over the Tyrrhenian Sea to the west, there was a faint ripple of wind, that traveled toward the land, across the gaping mouth of Father Tiber, past the port of Ostia where it tugged for a moment at the yards and sails of the merchantmen loading there. And finally on to die above the cauldron of Imperial Rome itself. Sweltering in the summer heat of the first year of the reign of the twelfth and last Caesar. Titus

Flavius Domintianus. Son of mighty Vespasian, and brother of the recently dead Titus.

The wind had just enough strength to flutter the stretched canvas over the Colosseum, sending waves of color across the great arena. A few of the people jammed into the rows of seats looked up at the noise, but most of them remained with their eyes fixed inexorably to the scenes in the bloody sand below them.

"I swear by all the gods that I cannot stand this damned heat a moment longer."

Poppaea nibbled irritably at a loose splinter of skin that hung raggedly at the side of her bitten nails. Although it was better for the sake of decency and propriety to be seen occasionally in public with one's husband, she was already regretting having suggested to dear Helvius that he should accompany her to the Games today.

"Then fan yourself, my sweetest hero. That is what others do."

Far below her, she watched idly as teams of slaves scampered from the arena, having removed all traces of the slaughter of animals that had taken place there during the morning. Poppaea was enamored of the savage delights of the Falvian Amphitheater and found that the day hadn't lived up, so far, to her expectations.

She could still remember the inaugural Games that Titus had held the previous year to celebrate the inauguration of the Colosseum. Now, that had been a real bloodletting. Even the special drainage system had found it hard to cope. At the thought of that colossal slaughter, the plump, middle-aged matron began to feel that delicious sweet moistness at the junction of her chubby thighs.

"Five thousand beasts killed that day," she said, half to herself.

2

"What?" said Helvius Geminus with mounting anger. The slaves who'd cleaned his second-best toga hadn't washed out all the urine they used as part of the whitening process, and he was conscious of the musty stale smell. But Helvius found a little consolation in the thought that among the stinking mix of other scents, there would hardly be anyone paying attention to him.

"Nothing my proud eagle. I was just remembering back to other happy days in your company."

Secretly she was hoping that her husband would decide that the heat and the crowd were all too much for him to stomach, and that he would leave her behind to enjoy herself in her own secret ways. There had been the bright-faced young boy from the family across the way from them. The last time they'd met at the Games, he'd taken advantage of her in the most wanton and shameless way. Unconsciously, Poppaea's fingers were plucking at the purple hem of her robe, ready to burrow under it and cool down that prickling heat that was beginning to overpower her.

"Sit still, Poppaea, or our neighbors will begin to think that you suffer from lice."

"Helvius!"

"I think that I shall be returning to our home, and I wish you to accompany me there."

"Where you are Gaius, I am Gaia," replied Poppaea, deliberately risking a further outbreak of rage from her husband by parodying the sacred marriage vows. But she knew Helvius well enough. One of the things that he loved about her was her willful flaunting of convention. But only in private, of course. He also liked the way his wife was happy to dedicate much of her time to her own private amusements, leaving him free to devote his time to his.

3

Like the little slant-eyed whore he kept in a small house on the eastern outskirts of Rome.

"There is a limit to the pleasure that I can derive from watching animals butchered."

"But after the showpiece with the lake it will be time for Vulpus."

The name sent a shudder of delicious pleasure through her plump body. The wonderful Vulpus. The Fox. The greatest fighting man in the history of the Games. That was what some men called him.

"Renegade Briton!" spat Helvius Geminus scornfully. Ever since Vulpus had made his first appearance in the arenas of Rome, his name seemed to have been on everybody's lips.

"No, my mighty warrior. He is no renegade."

"Father was a great man, who did the proper thing after he married that slut from Britain. Saxon or Celt or whatever she was."

"He is freeborn, Helvius. He fights for the Emperor."

"Fought for the Emperor, you mean. Now Titus has gone to his ancestors, Vulpus fights only for himself."

The argument had taken away the cloth merchant's decision to leave. If he were truthful, he was glad to have the chance to see the famous gladiator. Equally skilled with the sword or the net. A marvelous driver of horses. Instant death in the Games.

Helvius Geminus idly watched the scenes below him as the Colosseum was flooded ready for the next stage of the day's entertainment. Wrinkling his nose with distaste as his wife crammed another handful of honeyed dates into her round little mouth.

He thought back to what he knew of this Vulpus.

Marcus Julius Britannicus.

Now in his mid-twenties. Helvius had seen him two

4

or three times in the street or at the baths. A tall, finely built young man, his body heavily muscled and seamed with the pale lines of old scars. Father had been Lucian Julius. A military legate in Britannia. Forgot himself enough to wed a local woman. Some sort of princess by all accounts. Brought dishonor to his Legion.

"Twentieth Valeria Victrix, wasn't it?"

"Dear Vulpus's father's Legion? Yes it was. Why?"

He didn't bother to answer her.

The boy had been about fifteen, he'd taken the toga virilis Helvius thought, when his father had chosen to take note at last of what was said about honor and treachery. And had fallen on his own sword. And the mother?

"What happened to his mother? The British dam?"

"She was attacked and murdered by . . . , by someone or other. I just forget the truth of it, my dear."

Poppaea's evasion didn't check his thoughts. Yes. There had been talk of the killing, and there had been some high-ranking names linked to it. Something about . . . ? What was it? It slipped from him, and he cursed under his breath, wiping away a string of sweat from the side of his nose.

"Look!"

His wife's shrill cry was echoed from fifty thousand throats as the trumpets blared and the action began.

There had been something of Vulpus at that great red rock in the desert, where the Zealots had held out against Rome. Masada! That was the name of the rock. Helvius Geminus smiled in self-congratulation at his memory. And that mountain that had exploded, burying cities, must be two or three years back. Vesuvius. Pompeii. The tittle-tattle of the markets had placed Vulpus there as well. But there was always so much gossip built up round the top fighters. There was a rumor that Vulpus owed much of his early advancement to the Lady Agrippina, wife to that great darrel of a Tribune, Flavius Julius Germanicus. They said that the battles that Vulpus fought with her were of the sort that involved a deal of sweat but no bloodshed. Having met the lady in question several times, Helvius didn't envy the gladiator.

The orchestra began to play a soft, languorous love tune, the music echoing from the white stone walls. Although the Flavian Amphitheater had been open for better than a year, it was still immaculately clean.

Titus. The Emperor had taken a personal interest in Vulpus, and nothing eased the progress of a young man better than Imperial approval.

Boats were appearing from the opposing entrances, rowed by Nubians with polished skins, naked but for a small kilt of leather about their loins. Helvius felt his wife stiffen at his side, the pot of dates temporarily forgotten in her lap.

It had been in this very arena that Helvius had first seen Vulpus, but it had been a year or more back. Before the young man had made his name, becoming the idol of the fickle mob. Since then he had gone on from strength to strength. Had Vulpus been a slave, he would have been awarded the wooden rudis of freedom and his papers of manumission a dozen times over. Now here he was fighting something new and different. The Editor giving the Games had been cautious, letting it only be known that it would be a sight to remember, but not actually letting on what it would be. And the crowds had responded to his cunning.

The noise was falling as the spectators became involved in what was going on below them. Helvius had heard a rumor from a dye-peddler that Vulpus was to fight a woman giant they had discovered in a cave far to the east, who had three pairs of arms and four eyes.

The killing of animals had been rather boring, and the lunchtime slaughter of convicted criminals scarcely exciting enough to raise a howl from the crowd. Even when two men struck at each other simultaneously and both fell dead, there was hardly a ripple of laughter.

Now there was water. So it couldn't be the giantess. Helvius was a little disappointed. Particularly as the peddler had promised him that the woman had three separate vaginas. One under each arm and the third where her mouth should be.

The merchant gave a deep-throated chuckle at the idea.

There were ten boats. Long, narrow craft, with the blacks paddling from bow and stern, steering in toward the island that rose out of the murky water of the artificial lagoon that the engineers of the Colosseum had built. The sand and blood from the bottom of the arena was now covered by eight or ten feet of water, clearing slowly as the mud settled.

At the center of each boat was a long canopy, and the crowd buzzed with excitement as the covers were removed when the boats reached the orange hump of the island. Because each boat held five pairs of men.

Shackled together.

Right wrist to right wrist.

Helvius joined with Poppaea in the burst of cheering at the originality of the idea. So simple and so amusing. By chaining them like that it meant they were unable to fight side by side and must stumble together, swords clasped in their left hands.

"What will their opponents be?" exclaimed Poppaea, hoping secretly that it would be dwarfs. They

7

had seen dwarfs in the Colosseum only a month or so before, and she had been amazed at the strange proportions of the little men with their stunted legs. But they had fought naked. And she had seen with melting imagination that some of them had private parts that were quite out of proportion to their small bodies.

The men were all standing on the island, blinking uneasily in the strong light, some of them pulling each other to higher levels. Away from the water. The boats skimmed their way out of the arena, and the gates closed behind them.

The timing of the Editor and his minions was superb. If the reaction of the crowd was anything to go by, he was safely home in the election that was due in a week. His opponent would never be able to match this sort of spectacle.

Just as the mob were beginning to turn restless, waiting for the next scene in the drama, the trumpets gave another rousing, barbaric fanfare. The shadowed doors swung slowly open, and more boats came darting toward the island, propelled this time by light-skinned slaves. The boats were broader, with rowers rather than the paddles of the blacks. And each of the dozen boats had a heavy canvas awning set at its center.

Helvius Geminus had paid well for the seats near the front, only a few feet above the clearing waters. And from where he sat he felt the ripple of excitement. Under each awning sat a half-dozen naked girls. Black as jet, their skins glistening with oil and perspiration.

In the cheaper, higher rows, the crowd still couldn't see what was in the boats, destined to fight against the men who had now ranged themselves into a reasonable semblance of a defence on the island.

When, with a theatrical flourish, the coverings were thrown back and the girls, with a little prodding from the rowers, stood up, the roar from the mob was deafening. Helvius screwed up his eyes, wondering if it would ever cease. Poppaea screamed with the rest, bouncing to her feet, scattering dates all over the row in front, some of them actually plopping into the water of the arena. Her husband noticed that as she stood she left a damp patch on the pale stone of the seat, and he looked quickly away.

The girls were armed with gleaming short swords, modeled on the army gladius, but clearly lighter. They stepped out on edges of the island, some of them looking nervously back over their shoulders as the boats pulled away, leaving the water placid and still.

"Three to one for the men!" shouted a flushed-faced young man a few seats along to the left.

The betting erupted all around the arena, with most people favoring the men, despite their handicap.

"Fools! The women will cut those poor dogs down within minutes."

The speaker stood near one of the exits, looking down impassively at the scene far below him. He was tall, with black hair and brown eyes, unusual among Romans. His hair was cropped fashionably short, curling into the nape of his neck. There was the mark of a scar across his chin, and other scars dappling his upper arms like lace laid over flesh.

Unrecognized by the crowd, all with their eyes fixed on the coming battle, it was Marcus Julius Britannicus, called Vulpus.

An older man, his hair white and shoulders stooped, nodded agreement. "Should I lay odds for the women, Marcus?"

The gladiator didn't answer, easing the heavy metal

9

breastplate, rubbing his fingers across the pommel of his sword. It was almost as though he hadn't heard the old man's words.

"There are times that I hate this mindless hydra. They watch the killing and they gamble on it. Make money from suffering. Copulate later with the whores in the alleys below, their passions enflamed by blood."

"By Venus, Marcus! You sound like one of those damned Nazarenes. It has always been so."

Vulpus grinned. "Aye. That's so, brother. And always will be so. Yet I like it not. And I shall have none of it."

He turned away, ready to go down the steep stairs toward the chambers where he would undergo the final preparations for his part in the day. A part that would, if he lived, bring a large purse of gold to add to his savings.

The mob were there for every Games, and yet few of them had any knowledge of the skills involved. To imagine that these wretched prisoners from some squalid border conflict on the further edge of the Empire would stand a chance against the black bitches!

He knew the lanista who owned and trained the girls, and was aware of the price the Editor of today's Games was paying for them. They were skilled in killing, and formed a warrior clan which excluded men. Hated men.

"Unnatural, what they do, my dear Marcus," the lanista had whispered to him, laying a greasy hand on his sleeve that very morning. "I fear them myself."

Which was why, Marcus guessed, the man had agreed to what would happen later. A single gladiator could easily be disciplined if he became awkward. Or thrown quietly in the Tiber with a blade in his bowels.

But near a hundred women like these ...

Near a hundred women like that!

Helvius Geminus shifted in his cramped place, suddenly uncomfortably aware that the sight of these splendid black women with their red-tipped breasts was arousing him. His toga was rather tight and he moved his hand, letting his fingers brush against the swelling.

But women against men! It was ridiculous. Absurd.

"Absurd!"

"What?"

"I said that it's almost blasphemous to make these women fight against men."

Poppaea had reassembled her pot of dates, and stuffed three more at once into her mouth before mumbling an answer to her husband.

"The men are tied by the wrist, and they have their swords in their weak hands."

"But they have the vantage of the hill and . . . they are men."

It was a clinching argument, and one that Poppaea could not possibly refute. But she was enough of an expert in matters of the arena to suspect that the Editor might know more than the mob.

"A wager on it, Helvius my wondrous defender of all I hold dear?"

"Wager?" Had she suggested he might run naked through the Capitol he would hardly have been more surprised.

"I have this feeling, dearest Helvius, that the Gods will smile this day upon the weaker forces. I saw a brindled she-cat turn on a great black hound while walking in the garden this morning."

Which was a lie.

"Which is an omen! Really, Poppaea. What could we wager?"

"The villa on the Bay of Naples?"

11

"What of it?"

Below them, the action was nearly joined, but both of them were more interested in their own discussion.

"I asked that I might be allowed a black, or," she added hastily, "two blacks to help with the decoration. If the women should win, then you could allow me that?"

"And if they do not win?"

"Then the next time that your parents bless us with one of their interminable visits, I shall forbear to mention a certain house and certain lady who is being kept there by a certain man."

It was a crippling body-blow to poor Helvius Geminus. He had long suspected that his overweight wife was less faithful than Roman law demanded, but he had never looked for proof. Being less than interested in Poppaea's body. As long as she was discreet. There had been moments when he had wished for the great old days when a husband might slay a wife for infidelity.

Yet he had played his own game. And now was stunned to discover that his sleepy, idle wife knew of his mistress. And more, that she threatened to reveal it to his mother and father.

"I have left a letter with a close friend, Helvius, lest any mishap might befall me. The wager? Is it agreed?"

Helvius nodded wordlessly.

Poppaea smiled at him, honey from her dates dribbling down her chin. "Excellent. Then we are as one. We understand each other. And remember that letter, my dearest husband. You will, won't you?"

He nodded again. Uncertain as yet what had happened. And whether it was good or bad. Perhaps it was good. That they should lead their own discreet lives. As long as they were both careful.

Helvius resolved, before abandoning himself to the excitement of the Games, that he would be more discreet in future.

It was a sign of his caution that his mistress was found three days later in a back alley with her throat slit from ear to ear.

The men had arranged themselves in three rows, but the cunning of the shackling, right hand to right hand, was soon revealed. None of them wanted to be the one in the pair who faced away from the women, so there was constant movement among them, with them jockeying for position, pulling and pushing at each other. In one case rolling down the slope in a tangle, clean through the waiting women, to splash into the water.

The crowd cheered the action, quickly wagering on which of the men would remain above the lake longest. They fought and splashed, vanishing in white spray, watched by their fellows and by the black women. One of the pair realized that he was the weaker and would be tugged under first, so he thrust with his left hand, sinking the sword into his partner's belly. The man screamed, kicking away amid the spreading pool of crimson.

What the crowd spotted before the survivor was that as he died his corpse would simply drag the living man with it. And so it did.

But that was only a bonus for the mob, eager for the Editor to give the signal for the real fighting to begin. Reclining in his box, beaming from his wine-flushed face, the candidate for office judged his moment, then waved a negligent hand to one of his assistants. Who in turn nodded to another. Who

13

dropped his arm sharply to his side as the sign for the brassy notes of the trumpets to begin.

If the crowd had any area of complaint, it was that the fight lasted for such a short time.

Vulpus had walked down the maze of corridors, beneath the great stands, pausing only for a few moments to peer out through one of the windows. Seeing that things were going as he had expected.

The women chose to fight in pairs, each duo taking on one of the chained pairs of men. But the blacks had far greater mobility and they picked away at the men, forcing them to try and turn, blooding them almost at will.

Vulpus concentrated on one such fight, knowing that it was typical of the dozens of others scattered over the expanse of the sandy island.

The men were better than some, standing close in, shoulder to shoulder, refusing to be panicked by the leaping screaming women. Parrying their lunges as best they could. But the lithe black girls had every advantage. They were fighting unencumbered, and with their swords in their strong right hands. They were free to leap and circle, making the men shift and shuffle about, kicking up blinding red dust.

Inexorably, the flesh wounds began to tell, weakening the men. And their choice of the higher ground turned out to be yet another fatal decision against them. The women were able to stoop and cut at their legs, almost impossible to protect in the conflict.

Quickly, the one on the right of the pair that Vulpus was studying was slashed badly in the thigh. Probably hamstrung by the scream and the way his leg simply gave under him. His partner shouted out to him, the words utterly lost in the calls and jeers from the crowd, many of whom were losing a lot of money in misplaced wagers.

14

While the women stood off for a moment, watching their opportunity, the wounded man tried to haul himself to his feet, blood gushing over his legs and ankles, soaking into the sandy hillside. By leaning on the other man, he was just able to balance, waving the sword feebly with his left hand.

Vulpus shook his head.

"What would you have done?" asked the old man, standing by him.

"Had I been leading those poor doomed dogs?"

"Aye."

"I would have hit them as they stepped from their boats, when they were ill-prepared. Killed as many as possible and thrown them back into the water. Drowned the blood-crazed bitches."

He turned away, ready to finish his own preparations for his part in the climax of the day's Games. Behind him, in the arena, the fighting was nearly over.

The pair that Vulpus had been watching had gone down, with the black women attacking them simultaneously, risking a minor wound in order to lunge in and out, blood dripping from both their swords.

The roar of the crowd rose to a screaming climax as first the crippled man fell, slowly dragging down his partner, so that they both rolled awkwardly down the sandy slope, dappling it with their blood, finishing up in a tangled heap at the edge of the water.

Like most of the fifty thousand mob, Poppaea was on her feet, mouth hanging wetly open, revealing a double row of rotting teeth and three half-chewed dates. At her side, Helvius Geminus also somehow found himself up on his feet, yelling out the traditional "Hoc habet!" "Now he's had it."

One of the men tried desperately to raise himself up, cutting at the shackles that bound him to what was clearly a corpse, watching as the two women,

15

stalking like lithe black panthers, came slowly and inexorably toward him.

"Verbera!" screeched Poppaea. "Strike at him!"

Immediately in front of her an older woman was jumping up and down, the movement disturbing the front of her robe so that her left breast flopped out. There was a young man with her, his eyes dark-rimmed with kohl, who turned at the sight and, oblivious to everyone else, nuzzled at it voraciously.

"Iugula! Iugula!"

The cry of "Slay him! Slay him!" rose louder and louder, filling the baking Colosseum with its din.

Just before the female warriors got to him, the last surviving man succeeded in hacking himself clear of his partner, by the simple expedient of cutting through the dead man's arm, struggling to his feet. A sword in his left hand. And his right hand dangling an obscene ornament. A length of chain ending in a severed hand.

"Not fair! He's got three hands!" yelled someone several rows back, in the slaves' seats.

"Yes it is!" called someone else. "They've got four hands!"

The sally brought roars of laughter from the spectators. Helvius was oblivious to everything except those magnificent black bodies. The nipples hard at the tips of their firm naked breasts. Mouths hanging slackly open in a loose smile as they closed in on the bleeding man. Teeth gleaming like white spikes in the red caverns between their lips.

Helpless against the rising lust, the merchant touched himself, fingers clenching on his own manhood, unaware that men all over the Amphitheater were doing the same.

So were the women.

16

Sitting in the coolness below the arena. Marcus Julius Britannicus sat alone, absently honing the edge of his favorite sword, feeling the hilt warm to his hand. Listening to the din that echoed faintly down to him. Judging what was happening from the level of the noise. After the roars of excitement, he caught the change of pitch as things neared their climax. Fading away but with occasional loud shouts.

He guessed that the women had won easily, but there were possibly a few of the men still holding on and the mob were now waiting for that last surge of blood and death.

The woman hit the last man simultaneously.

One sword slid in under the waving left arm, splitting the flesh between the ribs, bursting the heart. As the woman called out in triumph, withdrawing the blade, it was followed by a spurting fountain of bright blood that splattered into the clearing water.

The second woman hit him from the other side, dodging the swinging chain and the dead hand, striking upward under the chin, through the jaw. Splintering his teeth, and pinning his tongue to the roof of the mouth. Up and through the soft palate until it tore into his brain.

The last man was dead before he even hit the ground, his arms spreading out, the chain splashing in the water, leaving the severed hand below the surface.

There was a second or two of near silence, and then uproar.

The crowd started to cheer, with some angry shouts from men who had lost their bets.

Poppaea turned to her husband. "That matter of the slaves for our villa, dearest hero?"

Helvius didn't answer her, being too busy watching with fascinated horror the activities of the naked

17

women in the center of the artificial lake. They were moving quickly from corpse to corpse. Bending down, a small silver knife gleaming in their hands. Pulling aside the cotton breeches of the dead men. Reaching under . . . tugging . . . slashing. Holding up their severed trophies to mock the crowd.

"Jupiter Optimus Maximus!" exclaimed Helvius Geminus. "The witches! By the . . . I cannot bear it."

Yet he still watched in the spreading pool of shocked and delighted silence that washed over the spectators as they saw the barbarous display of triumph.

His fingers still moved against himself, faster and faster, as he saw the tallest of the women make an outrageous and blasphemously obscene gesture with the genitals she had just hacked from one of the warm corpses.

The surface of the lake was dappled with splashes as the women threw away their trophies, grinning up at the crowd, who now howled their derision and hatred.

Poppaea stuffed another mouthful of honeyed dates into her wet mouth, panting with the excitement of the afternoon. So much killing, and there was still dear Vulpus to come. For a moment she wondered whether the Editor intended to match her hero with these naked savage women. Part of her hoped not, but there was another part of her that yearned for what such a battle might reveal.

If not the women, then what?

She felt warmth and wetness and stickiness beneath her and she stood up to ease herself, peering down into the calm waters. On the island, the women still stood together, waiting for the boats to come and ferry them back to safety.

The sun was glinting around the edges of the great

18

covering, gleaming off the dull water. Poppaea stared idly at the lake as she adjusted herself, ready to sit down again on the warm stone seats. She blinked as she saw . . . thought she saw . . . something moving under the surface. Something long and sinuous that sent an ominous greasy swirl to the water.

She shaded her eyes and looked again, but the reflection of the sun made it hard to see. Perhaps she'd imagined it.

Perhaps.

Followed by the old man, Vulpus strode among the echoing corridors, feeling the weight of the stones pressing down on him. Hearing the noise of the crowd almost shrunk to nothing. One of the Editor's assistants met them at a corner, clearly relieved that the star fighter was on his way and that there'd be no delay in the smooth running.

"Don't worry, boy. I'm here. Like I'm always here."

"I know. I know, Vulpus. But it was just that I thought I'd better . . ."

"Make sure I'd not run off . . ."

"No. No!"

"Is it nearly ready?"

"Yes, Vulpus. The girls won like you said they would. They won easily."

"You think they have won?"

"Of course they have won."

Marcus paused, checking his step suddenly so that the old man and the boy nearly tripped over him.

"They have lost."

TWO

It had long been one of Marcus's favorite pastimes to make up sayings for himself along the lines of some of the less proper Roman poets. And one of his favorite epigrams was that there were no endings—just a lot of beginnings.

Nowhere was that more true than in the arena. Particularly with the gladiatores meridiani who enlivened the lunchtime break. They were poor wretches of robbers and bandits who fought, if that was the correct expression, in pairs. But one would be armed and the other naked and weaponless. As soon as the armed man had slaughtered his hapless opponent, he in turn was stripped and had to face an armed man. So it went on, until there was only one survivor, who would be saved to open the proceedings on the next Games.

So it was today.

The women who had fought and beaten the armed

men, were themselves to be the victims. The crowd, from long experience, sensed this. But the black women, their bodies streaming with sweat, mingling in some cases with blood from minor flesh wounds, were innocent. Waiting in the broiling heat for their salvation.

It was not to be salvation, but it was to be an end to their part in the Games. Poppaea's eyes hadn't deceived her when she thought she saw movement deep within the waters of the artificial lake.

"Helvius!!"

Her husband, trying to find some way of sitting that would stop the wet patch at the front of his toga from sticking to him, jumped at the sudden scream. His wife was standing like a statue, the pot of dates in one hand, the other pointing at something in the lake.

The cry attracted everyone's interest, and almost immediately others saw it. Saw them. The shapes in the water. Moving silent and scaly green in the water, occasionally diving deep enough to stir up sand from the bottom of the arena. Fingers pointed and men and women stood again, craning to try and see just what the next surprise was to be.

"Fishes!" shouted one man.

A hundred voices taking up the cry. Then a thousand. The women on the island stood hushed, grouped together, their feet actually in the water, trying to make out what was happening. There were several of the creatures there, that was obvious. Waves were being stirred up, lapping gently at the stone walls, leaving a darker stain against the light dry areas.

The first attack by the creatures in the pool came and went so fast that few people actually saw it. There was an eruption of foam, white spray exploding in the air, and a glimpse of something vast and gray-green, and one of the black women had vanished, without even time to draw the breath for a scream. So fast that the girl who stood next to her scarcely moved.

"Pebble-worms!" shouted out a man close to Helvius Geminus. "They're lizard-fish!"

Crocodiles. Trapped by net from the eastern rivers of the Mediterranean, and transported in tanks of water in galleys to Rome by an enterprising bestiarius. They'd been seen before in the arena, and were always popular for their speed and efficiency as killers. These had been starved for days before the Games to make them faster to strike.

Unnoticed by any of the Nubian women, three, then four and five of the beasts had clambered out of the water on the far side of the island, and were slithering round toward the women, who still gathered near the edge of the lake, looking around and chattering to each other. Unable to believe that they weren't the victims of some dreadful mistake.

Only when they began to see other crocodiles heaving their way toward them did they begin to panic, some of them dropping their swords as they scampered back toward the top of the artificial island.

Where a half-dozen beasts were already waiting for them.

The Editor relaxed once more, a broad smile cloaking his thick lips, running a hand across his oiled hair as he listened in delight to the screams of the women, and the roars of the vast crowd. It was turning out even better than he'd hoped. And there was still Vulpus to come.

Yellow eyes unblinking, the crocodiles slithered their way across the carpet of corpses, pulling down woman after woman, dragging them down the slope and into the water. Already the lake had lost its clear depths. Now it was tinged here and there with red.

Gobbets of blood burst like some underwater plant across the surface of the pool, and hunks of flesh floated in the waves.

Vulpus watched, his face a mask of stone, as the women died. Although they were supremely disciplined against other humans, these unearthly saurians had destroyed their nerve, and they ran and died as any ordinary Roman housewife would have done.

The bestiarius had claimed that he was going to release eighty of the monsters into the flooded arena, which probably meant around thirty, if he was like other animal trainers that Vulpus had known.

Marcus scanned the Amphitheater from behind the bars of the grating, locking off the arena from the maze that lay behind and under the giant new Colosseum. Looking for the monster that he had been readying himself for. So far, it had not appeared, lurking in the deeps, waiting its moment to appear.

There was a lot of noise from the mob on the far side of the island to him, with men and women standing and pointing at something. That something finally appeared over the top of the dusty hill, pausing like some eastern potentate surveying his territory. It was easily the biggest crocodile that Marcus had ever seen. A full eight paces long, wearing a collar of silver studded with semiprecious uncut stones that glittered in the sunlight.

One of the women saw it, and turned to run down the slope, but she tripped in her panic, falling on her face, landing on top of one of the mutilated corpses, her sword spinning into the bloody water. The beast saw her and went after her. In a chilling waddling rush, its feet churning powerfully down the slope, jaws gaping, revealing the rows of yellow teeth.

The Nubian girl managed to get to her feet just a

split fraction of time before it reached her, and tried to dodge sideways. But it was fast.

"Mithras! It's fast!" exclaimed Marcus to nobody in particular.

In midrush it swiveled, locking those jaws like an iron trap around the woman's ankles. Marcus had seen the great lizards before, and was ready for the next move.

The crocodile kills most of its victims by drowning, rather than biting or swallowing them. This Emperor among creatures was no exception. It rolled, bracing its stubby legs, keeping its teeth buried in the girl's flesh, bringing her down almost on top of it, her arms flying up as she fought for her balance. But she had no chance against a monster that size, and its roll took it into the shallows on the edge of the island.

With great bravery one of the black warriors that had not given in to the general fear saw it, and ran across, her sword raised. Hitting it a cracking blow across the top of the head, just behind the shuttered eyes. She could as well have swatted it with a feather fan. Although the crowd cheered her courage, it was a futile gesture. The great beast rolled once more, dragging the struggling girl under with it in a welter of blood and froth.

Interested, Marcus watched to see if the creature would reappear, either with or without the victim, but it disappeared totally. The bestiarius had told him that the crocodile was able to stay under water for a great time without needing to come up again to breathe. They had drunk together the night before, each admiring the professional expertise of the other, but each taking great care not to give away any secrets.

The bestiarius, a man from the east, was justifiably proud of the way he'd trained the lizards. Normally they would prefer to take dead meat, but he had managed to teach them to attack only the living and ignore corpses. And to stop them after the kill trying to cache away the body until it reached the required degree of putrefaction.

"I was given a couple of hundred of those damned Nazarenes to practice on," he had boasted. "Better than cattle and a lot less expensive. Cost me only eight aurei for the whole lot. My beauties went through them all in a couple of weeks. All it took. Couple of weeks."

Marcus had nodded wisely, remembering a young girl he had once met back in cold Britannia. She had been a Nazarene, called Gwenhwyvar, though she said her new name was Mary.*

Several of the women chose to try their luck with the water, rather than wait for the rending death that stalked the small island. Most of them weren't able to swim, and the cheaper seats soon rang to wagers on which bobbing black head would disappear next.

Marcus rubbed the line of grease over the eyes, smeared there to check perspiration from running into his eyes. An old fighting trick that one-eyed Argos had taught him as a young boy back home across the sea. One of the girls was swimming strongly, only a few paces from the safety of one of the ledges above water level, when something struck her from below, hurling her body clear of the murky, red-tinged lake.

She screamed once, then splashed down out of sight, reappearing held in the jaws of the monster crocodile, its distinctive collar showing it as the leader of the pack. It shook the Nubian woman as a dog shakes a rat, her arms and legs flailing helplessly. back and forward, to the great amusement of the mob. Fi-

---

*See *The Land Of Mist*, also available from Pinnacle Books.

nally, holding her around the thighs, the beast dragged her under.

Although Marcus studied the spot, the corpse didn't float as a normal body would.

It wouldn't be long.

There were only a handful of the women left alive actually on the island, trying to make some kind of a fight against the circling, patient, knob-backed ring of monsters. But their light swords were little use against the heavy armor of the crocodiles, merely provoking them into their shuffling charges that inexorably took a girl with it.

One girl dived courageously on top of one of the lumbering saurians, stabbing at its eyes, succeeding in blinding it, but it rolled, crushing her under its weight, snapping her up in its jaws, and dragging her ponderously toward the waiting depths. Her voice, shrill with nameless agony, rose over every other noise, and she clawed at the sandy ground to try and stop the monster's progress. Her nails bent and broke, and the end of her fingers bled raw.

But she still ended her life with lungs full of blood and sand and water.

Suddenly, it was over.

Just as the women had wiped out the men, so they in turn had all fallen victim to the greedy reptiles. The victorious crocodiles prowled the island, snapping at bodies, making sure that nothing lived there. Marcus watched and waited. His turn was nearly come.

Boats skimmed out again from the concealed entrances, manned by men with skins the color of fine oil. Small men, wearing unusual head dresses of cotton, that tumbled into a veil at the nape of the neck. Marcus saw that his bestiarius drinking friend directed them from a larger boat, pointing and calling, until

26

they were in the positions he wanted. Then, at a signal that Marcus didn't catch, the men began to beat at the scummy water with the flat of their paddles, churning it up into a fetid froth, the slapping noise quietening the spectators.

There was movement under the water, and Marcus saw how well the trainer had done his work. The great reptiles were leaving the arena, vanishing through the gates below the level of the lake like a well-drilled band of murderers. One small accident marred the perfection of the operation, causing the Editor to sit up anxiously, spilling the wine from his costly glass goblet.

On its way out, one of the crocodiles lashed out at a small boat with its armored tail, upsetting it and tipping the four men into the water. Other boats paddled in close enough to pick up three out of the four. But the last one was unlucky. Perhaps he had not prayed long enough to whatever god he worshiped.

The beast that had upset the boat came up under him, locking his head and shoulders in its death grip, ready to dive and end his existence. Which would have been fast and not too unpleasant as violent deaths go. But his luck was truly out.

Another crocodile was attracted by the screams and commotion and managed to lock its teeth into the wretched man's legs, tugging him in the opposite direction.

Poppaea glanced down at her sweetmeats, and was somewhat disappointed to see there were only five more rich sticky dates left. But Vulpus . . . her beloved Vulpus, would soon be making his appearance. When she looked up she joined in the hoots of merriment at the sight of the slave with his head gripped in one set of teeth and his legs in another, being tugged clear out of the water.

27

"Like Domitian between two of his whores!" shouted out a daring spectator somewhere around to their left. A sally that brought cheers from the crowd and an angry glance from the Editor.

"More like you with two of your blacks, Poppaea, my dearest dove," hissed Helvius Geminus in her ear.

"The wager was won, Husband. I shall leave for the Bay of Naples the day after tomorrow."

They both smiled thinly and politely at each other, turning away to watch the events in the flooded Amphitheater. The two crocodiles dived simultaneously under the lake in a welter of bloody foam. And reappeared some distance apart. The one still held the head and shoulders between its grinning jaws. The other, thirty paces away, held the rest of the body.

The Bestiarius was worried by the delay and blew a small golden whistle, its thin, clear note piercing the noise of the arena. All of the saurians vanished under the water, and the great artificial lake was still.

The slaves paddled quickly to the island and hurriedly cleared it of the tangled mass of bodies, heaving them into the water, where they plopped and hung together in a messy heap. Marcus tutted his irritation. Although it would have taken too long to clear them properly, it still looked sloppy. Untidy. Unprofessional.

Then the men scampered back to their frail boats and paddled out of the arena again, leaving only the larger vessel of the bestiarius himself near one side of the lake, under the box of the Editor.

Waiting for the signal. It came in the form of a blast on the trumpets. And the main gate opened and out slid an ornate boat, enameled on its flanks, with six pairs of oarsmen, tugging at their gilded blades.

And in the prow, wrapped in a cloak that glittered in the sun, stood the erect figure of . . .

"Vulpus! Vulpus!! Vulpus!!!"

"Vulpus!!!! Vul . . ." Poppaea tried to eat the last handful of dates and call out the name of her idol all at the same time. The result was predictable.

She choked.

Eyes popped like grapes in a vat of dough. Jaw worked and gobbled, blood swelling in the arteries and veins of her neck and face. Clawed at Helvius Geminus, who at first shrugged her off angrily, then turned back with more concern as he saw her plight.

Bad though elements of their marriage might be, and though there had often been times when he had wished her dead—the last time being two minutes earlier—it was still not possible to sit among their friends and neighbors and simply allow his wife to choke to death.

Helped by other spectators, stirred by the unexpected action, Helvius half-carried, half-dragged his spluttering wife out of the aisle to the cool and calm of the shaded corridor. Laying her down and patting her cheeks to try to help her, while a crowd materialized from nowhere and ringed them.

Out in the brightness of the afternoon, he heard the ringing cheers for Marcus Julius Britannicus and cursed his greedy wife for spoiling what promised to be a combat to remember in the sun-baked Colosseum.

Vulpus was oblivious to the suffering state of one of his most fanatical admirers. He was locked into his own thoughts, trying to control his breathing, balancing easily with his legs apart in the center of the barge. The cheering went on and on, but it sounded only like the muted hum of lazy summer bees in a river meadow. All in his mind was closed in on the task in hand.

The bestiarius watched him nearing the island, then gave another signal. A series of shrill blasts on his whistle, then he muttered something to his own oarsmen who paddled him quickly from the arena and out of sight.

Bracing his foot against the forward thwart, Marcus jumped lightly and easily from the boat on to the furrowed, bloodsoaked sand of the artificial island at the center of the Amphitheater, throwing off his cloak, and hearing the cries of "Vulpus!" double and redouble. Flinging it casually to a man in the boat.

The Emperor had given him that cloak with his own hands, he thought vaguely. Not Domitian who now ruled Rome. But his elder brother Titus who had plucked Marcus from relative obscurity and helped to make him what he had now become. The most famed gladiator in the Empire.

After the coolness, the heat on the island was stunning. Hardly helped at all by the water that lapped greasily at the sandy edges. He looked with distaste at the rocking tangle of bodies at the corner of the arena. White men and black women mangled together in death, embracing each other so closely with a hideous parody of affection.

It was time to move for the high ground, before his opponent got there first. On the slippery slopes, it might be fatal to be there too late.

Sword ready in his hand, the light armor that he had chosen for the fight fitting him smooth as a second skin, Marcus reached the top of the hill, and stood there surveying the ground. Noting where the sand was rutted, and where several bodies had bled and formed a pool of clinging red mud.

Only then, pausing for a moment, did he look up

and around him. Gazing up and up at the towering achievement that was the Flavian Amphitheater. Many years in the building, he had first seen it in detail only a year and a half ago, after the burning deaths of Pompeii.*

Then it had been incomplete, and the host of memories of that time came flooding back to him, unbeckoned. Faces and bodies. Living and dead.

Now he stood truly alone, the boat that had brought him vanished in safety. The memories of the last year and a half thronged about him, even as the roar of the mob told him that his opponent had at last put in an appearance. Slowly, he turned to face the monster crocodile, its collar glittering at its scaly neck, as it crawled ponderously out of the bloody water toward him.

---

*See *City of Fire*, also available from Pinnacle Books.

THREE

It had begun toward the end of the first year of the Emperor Titus. Titus Flavius Vespasianus. Only days after the horrors of erupting Vesuvius.

Through the intervention of the Tribune Flavius Julius Germanicus, cuckold husband of the insatiable Lady Agrippina,* Marcus had been granted an interview with the Emperor in his palace in Rome.

Titus had the sharp eyes of his father and the erect bearing of the soldier he had been. He was greatly interested in the young man standing before him. The history of Marcus's family was all too well known in Rome, but the Emperor made no reference to it. Though Marcus was constantly expecting some word of his disgraced father and his dead mother. Raped and butchered by the flower of aristocratic Rome. There were moments that Titus seemed about to

*See *Hill of the Dead*, also available from Pinnacle Books.

speak more than the conventional pleasantries, yet held his tongue.

They had talked about Masada, and both remembered the heat and the bravery of the Zealots. And of fighting. Titus was greatly interested in what Marcus knew of fighting. The young man wondered how he was so well known. But it was not a question to ask your Emperor.

Finally, Titus stood up to indicate the audience was over, and asked Marcus what help he might give him. It was a hard moment. To have the favor of the Emperor shine upon you could open doors. Fill your purse with gold. Achieve advancement in the Army or the Senate.

But there was something that Marcus wanted more than any of those things.

Vellius Condorus!

The last survivor of the band of rich young Romans who had found it great sport to assault, rape and then butcher a Princess of the Iceni and steal her gold. There had been eight men involved to some degree or other.

Eight men. Proud and arrogant in their position and their wealth.

Seven were dead.

While he listened to the formal words of the Emperor, Marcus mentally ticked them off in his mind.

Flavius Paulinus.

Publius Salvius.

Maecilius Severus.

Julius Priscus.

Metellus Curtius.

Suetonius Postumus.

Fat old Crassus.

All dead.

And Vellius Condorus.

He still lived. His presence a constant flame that blazed in Marcus's mind.

Vellius Condorus. The subprocurator in Britannia. With authority over the Dumnonii.

A big man, running to fat. Round head set squarely on a thick neck. Balding, like a goose's egg. A coarse, spoilt face, with red-rimmed eyes that could betray his rages like a wild pig.

"I am waiting, Julius Britannicus."

The Emperor's words snapped him back to the present. He bowed slightly, racking his brains for what Titus had last been saying.

"I wish to return to the land of my birth."

"Britannia?" Again there was something there. The suspicion that there was more left unsaid than said.

The thought of being able to reach Vellius Condorus and reap from his the vengeance the others had given him had made him tremble slightly. It was as though a red veil had been drawn across his eyes.

The memories of those mangled corpses of the other killers. Torn and broken. Ripped apart. Entombed. Burned alive. Drowning in stinking vomit. Castrated and blinded.

Those seven men had already paid a high enough price for their treatment of his mother. One more and the toll was ended.

"Aye. If it pleases you, my Emperor, then it will please me to go. Perhaps as your . . . envoy?"

He let the last word hang, so that it would be clear what he meant. The higher a man rose in Imperial Rome, the more he would fear plotters. Conspiracies. The knife in the groin and the smiling man with the blade beneath the toga. Titus would understand that he meant 'spy' though he said 'envoy.'

The Emperor nodded, quickly making up his mind. It were better to have this Marcus Julius Britannicus as an ally. And there were whispers of discontent in that cold island to the north. A man born there would be better than a pampered young Tribune.

So it was.

Marcus smiled as he left the Imperial Palace, heading for the busy docks and a ship bound for Britain.

He heard feet running after him when he was only a few hundred paces from the Palace, and he stepped quickly aside, turning into a small shop selling bowls and dishes in poor quality pottery, his hand dropping automatically to his sword. His father had once told him that a man who supped with an Emperor should make certain he had clean fingers. It wasn't unknown for a dinner guest to fall prey to footpads on his way home from an Imperial banquet.

"Honored sir. How truly wonderful that your magnificence had deigned to honor this humble person's establishment with your presence. Bringing light into the dull and dark world that I am forced to inhabit. Perhaps you desire a small present for a lady or ... Aaaargh!"

The point of Marcus's sword brought a thread of blood worming from the shopkeeper's scrawny neck, pinning him back against a stand of pots, making it teeter and rock alarmingly.

"One more word and you join your stinking ancestors today instead of tomorrow," hissed Marcus, peering under the stained awning across the front of the miserable little shop. Listening for the noise of feet.

Which had stopped.

There was the noise of the street. A donkey braying and a slap from its owner. A woman crying somewhere in an upstairs room. A couple of small children quarreling over a wooden doll.

"Marcus Julius Britannicus! I bear a message for you from the Emperor! Marcus Julius Britannicus!"

Assassins rarely announced themselves as messengers from the Imperial presence, but Marcus kept a tight hold on his gladius as he stepped from the shop, leaving the owner a fainting heap in the corner. To the smells of the street was added the unpleasant odor as the man fouled himself in fear.

The man who had called out his name was still standing near the corner of the street, back turned, looking anxiously around.

"Marcus Julius Britannicus!" There was a note of panic entering his voice.

"I am he," said Marcus, stepping silently up behind the man, making him jump a clear foot in the air.

Fear of failure had made the man's face somehow smudged and unfocused. Sweat dribbled down the bridge of his narrow nose, gathering under his chin. His barber had nicked him while shaving that morning and there was the remains of a pad of cotton stuck to his chin with dark dried blood.

"Marcus Julius Britannicus?"

"Why are you following me?"

The man shook his head, sending sweat splattering into the dry dust. "No. No, my master. I bring word from the blessed Emperor who desires a further audience with you."

"He has just dismissed me with a commission to travel to Britain."

"He wishes only to see you again," said the man, still trying to regather his dignity and his breath. He leaned a hand against the wall of a house to remove a stone from his sandal while he looked at Marcus.

"When?"

"Now."

36

As they walked through the trees and bushes of the gardens of the Palace Titus rested his hand gently on the arm of the broad-shouldered young man. Song birds fluted and fountains played and danced.

"I have arranged for food to be brought out here in the open, so that we may eat as we talk. And as we talk we shall be sure out here that we are not overheard. Within those walls, there are too many ears."

The Emperor led Marcus to a large glade, surrounded by stately trees, with a stream running through it, and a shaded pool where carp glided among the reeds. A table stood at the center of the hollow, loaded with platters of food and amphorae of wine nestling in bowls of mountain snow. Slaves stood about the table ready to serve their master and his guest, but Titus sent them scurrying off with a wave of his hands. Seating himself on one of the two couches by the table, motioning Marcus to make himself comfortable on the other.

There were plates of olives. Mice rolled in honey and dipped in poppy seeds. Crabs. Peahen's eggs. Slices of roast pig and calf. Fish to dazzle the palate, including the rare red mullet. Lobsters cooked with beans and lettuces. Goose's liver garnished with small mushrooms and asparagus.

Marcus picked carefully at the rich selection, and sipped at the goblet of wine that the Emperor pressed on him, wary of any form of overindulgence. Wondering why Titus had sent after him.

"You wonder to find yourself back here again so soon, do you not?"

"I do, my Emperor."

"It is not only women who are always changeable, Marcus. It is also the prerogative of the wearers of the Imperial purple. After you had gone, I pondered on what we had said. And on what we left unsaid, and I decided we would talk a little more. Privily, with no man here but you and I. Do you begin to understand?"

Marcus didn't, but he nodded wisely, sipping his watered wine to prevent himself having to give a more revealing reply to the question.

"I thought so. Your reputation is well-earned. I knew your father, Marcus. A fine man, I thought him, though there were others who did not."

He paused, and Marcus saw that this time he would have to make some sort of answer. "I never knew of any reason why my father should have chosen to end his life so."

"Ah. Did you not? There were few who did. I have only learned of it lately. A slave, from the household of . . . let us just say a slave . . . was being questioned in my presence when he revealed something of the way that Lucian Julius Britannicus, your father, was hounded to his death."

"Hounded!"

Long nights for many years, the boy who had been Marcus had laid awake. At first weeping silently, then as he grew older, angry and puzzled, at being the son of a traitor. His mother had never told him the details, and he had never dared ask any other person. All he knew was that there was talk of some sort of treachery, involving his father's marriage to a non-Roman. Unable to refute the charges, his father had fallen on his sword.

That was all he'd ever known. Only now did he realize that in his heart of hearts he had come to believe that his father must actually have been guilty.

But now . . . !

"Yes, Marcus, my boy. I now know that the charges against your father were fabricated. False. But so skillfully were they laid that he could only twist and wriggle in their net, drawing it more tightly around himself."

It was like being struck over the head with a butcher's cleaver. Years rolled away and he saw again his father's face. Stern and unsmiling. Telling him that there was only one way that a noble Roman could deal with the situation. He asked the boy, barely in his teens, to look after his mother and to honor their forebears. That had been the last time that Marcus had seen his father.

Alive.

He stood up, facing the Emperor, so angry and blinded by the mixture of emotions that he almost committed the ultimate sacrilege and drew his sword in the face of Titus. He saw the shrewd eyes narrow, as though he read his thoughts.

"Once take out your gladius here, and you are a dead man, Marcus," the Emperor warned him, never raising his voice above the normal conversational tone.

Marcus swallowed hard, fighting a desperate battle to bring himself under control. Titus watched him closely, nibbling on a slice of fowl, throwing the bone on the grass.

"Well, Marcus? I cannot pass a whole day with you, pleasant though your company is."

"Who? Just tell me the names of the men, my Emperor. That is all I ask."

"It is no more than you deserve. But first, I wish to talk a little more about you. Your mother was killed by some Romans in Britain." It wasn't a question. A simple statement of fact. "You agree?"

Marcus stood silent.

"Very well. At least you don't disagree. I have compiled a list of the men involved in the dastardly crime. It had been my intention to punish them. Can you imagine what my agents have told me?"

Marcus wondered if he should deny any knowledge of the matter. Then, looking Titus in the eyes, he saw that it would be better not to try and dissemble with this man. Unlike some of his predecessors at the head of the Empire, Titus was not a fool.

"They are all dead."

"All but one. Where was it you wished to go when we met earlier? Britain, was it not? Let me see. I am sure that I know the name of a certain subprocurator there. It couldn't have any . . ."

"Vellius Condorus. And yes, my Emperor, I would have slain him as I have slain the other dogs. Now . . ."

"Now?"

"You know that I have served you well and with loyalty. I have served Rome as my father before me. My life is in your hands."

Titus clapped his hands softly together in mock applause. "A brave speech, Marcus, my dear boy. But do remember that your life is *always* in my hands. You are good at killing those you hate?"

"There is no greater pleasure, my Emperor."

"Well enough. I have decided that I wish to make myself better loved by my people. All my reforms and care for them is as a burned feather in the balance set against the fact that I have no champion in the Games. You will be that champion for me. Marcus Julius Britannicus."

It was a second thunderbolt.

"But I . . ."

"You what?" There was a thin note of anger in the voice of the Emperor. "You have butchered seven members of the great families. If even a whisper of this leaked out, as one day it must, then your life is not worth a stuffed capon. Unless . . ."

"Unless I have your protection, my Emperor."

Titus smiled. "Come sit beside me. I hate having to

40

look up to you like this. It is not a position I find that I am used to. There. You imagine that I will force you to fight for me and in return I will take you under the Imperial shadow. To keep you from the beaks of hawks. Is that not what you think?"

"It is."

Titus laughed. Threw back his head and bellowed with fullblooded mirth, the explosion of noise bringing a dozen armed men at the run. Wiping tears from his eyes he waved them all away again, smiling at Marcus.

"By Mercury, but that is as honest a word as I have heard since I came to the purple. You are no flattering courtier, with honey dripping from your tongue and poison in your ring." The smile vanished. "Marcus. That tongue pleases me, because I believe that it doesn't lie. But if you enter my service then you must guard it better. An Empire can fall to a careless word as easily as to a mighty army."

"I will, my Emperor."

"More wine? No? Well. I swear by Mercury, because he is the God for merchants and all who are dealers. I am a dealer, Marcus. And I shall deal with you. This is my offer. You will go as my man to be trained as a gladiator. You will learn all the skills. I know that some are known to you. You will better them. Sword, bow, javelin. Horse, chariot. Net. Dagger. You will learn them all. As the fighting man of Titus. In return you will have my protection. Is that a bargain?"

Marcus lay out on the ornately carved bench, rubbing a finger across a gilded figure of a little naked boy riding astride a dolphin. Wondering what to answer.

"My Emperor. If I agree, then you will, I think, have the better of the bargain."

The whisper hardly disturbed the air, so quietly did Titus speak. "Aye, truly Marcus. Yet the other side of such a coin is to die in darkness and alone. My arm is long, Marcus. And my eye never sleeps."

"The men who disgraced my father?"

"I was coming again to that. To travel straight forward is not always fastest."

"To turn aside from the path is to fall among wild beasts."

"Don't chop epigrams with me, Marcus!" The note of anger and authority was there again, and Marcus noted it well.

"I will be your man, my Emperor. And I will train to fight for you."

"In return I will protect you, so that you are known as my man. There may be times . . ." again the voice dropped to a whisper. "There may be times when I will look to you for your skills outside the Amphitheater. You understand me, Marcus, do you not?"

Titus meant that he should also become his killer. His tidier of messes. His remover of obstacles. To be a gladiator was one thing. To be a paid assassin was another.

The Emperor judged his moment to perfection. "For that, I give you more than I have said. Swear your sword to me, and I will give you names."

"My . . . !"

"The men who caused the death of your father."

"How many?"

"Four. Will you swear?"

Marcus laid his hand on the hilt of his gladius, feeling it cool to the touch. Knelt off the couch, on the grass beside the table. "I swear that I shall be your man. That I will fight for you."

"At any time and in any place," prompted Titus,

glancing around to make sure they were not overlooked.

"At any place and at any time," finished Marcus, rising to his feet.

The Emperor smiled. "I could not have made a better choice. And now you shall have the names. I will say them once and once only. Then never again. Is that understood?"

Marcus nodded.

"Well. They are Gaius Cassius Isidorus. Metellus Julius Vitruvius. His cousin, Lucius Julius Gellius."

"That is three, my Emperor. You said four."

Titus smiled broadly. "I give you pleasure here. You may slay two ducks with the one slingshot. The fourth is Vellius Condorus."

"Mithras! I know the others slightly. All of them live here in Rome. But Condorus. That double whoreson bastard! He is a thousand miles away."

"I reward those who please me, as you please me, Marcus Julius Britannicus. The orders that I shall make tonight will include one of interest to you. It will tell a certain subprocurator that the Emperor requires his presence here and that he must leave Britain immediately. Vellius Condorus will be in Rome within the month."

Condorus. In Rome. Marcus smiled.

It had been a good day.

FOUR

"Dearest Marcus. Would you think me quite outrageous if I asked you again to unsheath your mighty weapon and plunge it into me right the way to the hilt?"

The Lady Agrippina. Wife to the great barrel of a Tribune, the rich Flavius Julius Germanicus. In earlier adventures, Marcus had saved her life in an attack by Jewish Zealots. And Agrippina was not one to forget a face and a favor. Though in the case of Marcus, it was hardly his face that particularly interested her. Her husband had helped out Marcus on more than one occasion, making him welcome when they met. It had actually been Germanicus who had taken the young man to meet Titus a few days earlier.

Marcus wasn't sure if the Tribune knew of his wife's lechery. He thought that he did, and hoped that he didn't. But he was wise enough in the ways of decadent upper-class Rome to know that it was rare for a patrician lady not to have a lover. Even a string of them. While the men went their own way among a positive army of kept women.

Germanicus was off hunting in the hills to the north and wasn't expected back for three or four days. Marcus was glad that his break from the training school was only for a day and a night. Longer than that and the insatiable lady would have worn him to a thread.

"Show me what weapon drill you have been learning. Now that you are the Emperor's man, you must have become even better with your great sword."

He reached across the tumbled bed and gripped her right breast hard between finger and thumb, squeezing it cruelly so that the nipple rose like a ripe cherry, and she moaned and writhed, her own fingers reaching for him. Scratching across his flat muscular stomach, burrowing among the mat of jet black curling hair, until they reached their target, and gripped him. As Agrippina ran her fingers up and down the shaft, he winced at the scraping from her rings. Chunky ornaments of great value and little beauty.

The weather had taken a turn colder, and the shutters over the great doors to the garden of their town house had been closed.

Marcus let go of her breast, glancing across to see that his finger had left a white weal just beneath the nipple. He leaned across and bit her hard on exactly the same spot. Making her yelp her delight and pain.

"My hero! You must not mark me like that! If any of the slaves should see."

"Let them see, my delightful lover," he said with a bravado that he didn't actually feel. He had heard of too many tolerant husbands forced finally to take action over a servant's gossip.

Her head rolled on the bed, disturbing her tightly

45

packed curls. "Please, Marcus, Please. I beg you to bury it in me. As deep as a cavern and deeper yet."

She wriggled her chubby thighs apart, pulling him toward her. Guiding him in and clamping her legs in the small of his back to pull him in even deeper. Nothing loath, Marcus thrust as hard as he could, feeling himself make a jarring contact far within her that almost made her faint away with the agony and with the ecstasy.

Despite her age—Agrippina must be well past thirty—she was an excellent, if somewhat demanding, partner in the games of love.

As he worked at her, taking some of his weight on his elbows, her tongue snaked out and licked the runnels of perspiration from the hollow of his neck, her hands roaming across his back. Nails digging in to him.

"Careful! I was cut by a damned Thracian and the salt's still in it!"

"And what happened to the Thracian?" panted the Lady Agrippina.

"He died," said Marcus.

It had been a damned odd business, about that Thracian. He had been shortish. Shoulders like an ox. A puckered scar over the left eye and several other healed wounds webbed across his body. Clearly a fighting man of some experience, skilled in the arts of the arena.

He had been one of many men in the school that Marcus had been sent to. The Ludus Magnus, built by stammering Claudius, out on the Via Labicana. A great rambling fortress of a place, where a man could learn all there was to know about winning.

And dying.

The lanista, or trainer had once ruled supreme. He

had collected the men to fight. The animals. Everything that was needful for the running of the Games.
Out in the country and in the provinces they still plied
their trade, but not in Rome. In Rome the men who
counted were the Procuratores. Men who acted as official agents, and who controlled every aspect of the
recruitment and training of the gladiators. The head
Procurator was a tall skinny man, named Antonius Tiberius Scipius, and he had accepted Marcus into his
school with a deal of bowing and scraping. Which
went on until Marcus had to specifically ask him to
treat him quite ordinarily. Let him live and mix with
the others.

And they were a fine raggle-taggle bunch. Prisoners
from all frontiers of the Empire, hoping to win
through and achieve citizenship. Bought slaves, and a
small number of ruined sons from good families who
sought either fame or death. None of them minded
which.

The days of training seemed to Marcus, looking
back on them, to be a blur of action and exhaustion.
With certain moments standing out more clearly than
others. And, as he'd told Agrippina, the strange in-
dicent with the Thracian stood out more clearly than
any other.

It had been on only the fourth day of training. The
gladiators who taught them the skills were all grizzled
veterans who'd either been good enough or lucky
enough, to survive. Most of them had lost fingers. In
one case an arm. And one of the archery instructors
stumped around on a leg and a half.

The morning had been exercises designed to speed
up your reflexes. Like running along a narrow path
dodging among swinging great spheres of iron,
studded with spikes. While men thrust at you with
staves tipped with blunted points.

47

The Thracian had positioned himself at the very end of the line, opposite to a great giant of a man from the Northlands. Most of the slaves stood in fear of him, and even Marcus muttered a quick prayer against the evil eye when he first met him.

It wasn't the man's great height—a clear hand's span over Marcus—but the face and hair. The face was white and seeming bloodless. Hewn from a wind-washed bone with hollows scraped out where the eyes should be. The hollows filled with glowing embers of fire that smoldered redly. And the hair was a tumbling cascade of silver. Fine as the finest thread that could be woven it hung to the man's shoulders like a mane of spun ice.

His name was Ragnar. That was all the name he would own to. He had been captured in a skirmish above the line of snow, far, far to the north, where a man's breath smoked in the air and a gob of spittle would crackle and freeze in seconds on the iron ground.

He spoke a barbarously accented Latin, and kept himself to himself in their training quarters. Twice Marcus had been matched against him in mock conflict and had been amazed at the man's speed and strength. If Ragnar lived through to fight in the arena he would be a sensation.

Marcus felt a strange kinship with this lonely man. Both were outcasts in their own way. And both men were feared by the others in the camp. Ragnar for his height and power and inhuman appearance. Marcus Julius Britannicus because of his skill with arms. His doubtful temper. And because it was commonly known that he was the Emperor's man. Destined for other things.

If he lived.

It was common for rich patricians to drop into the

Ludus Magnus on their way to one or other of the baths, and this morning there was the usual gaggle, watching the men as they dodged and fought, trying to pick out those who would be worth a few aurei when they reached the arena in a couple of weeks.

The Procurator was standing in the training area himself, bellowing at the men as they worked out, cursing anyone who was too slow in ducking the iron balls. Marcus was standing by him waiting his turn, when he realized that he was the center of attention for the group of nobles over to the left.

"Who are they?" he asked curiously.

Tiberius Scipius peered across, his skinny neck poking out like a heron seeking fish. "Patrons. The one on the left is a great gambler on gladiators. His name's Gaius Cassius Isidorus. That one."

Marcus had learned to school his feelings and he stared around at the onlookers with no more concern than if he had been picking out a field slave. The one on the left. That one. A man who was distinguished by one main thing. He was so totally undistinguished. Had he turned away, Marcus could have remembered nothing about him.

Conscious of Marcus's gaze, Isidorus whispered something to one of the others who laughed dutifully. Marcus clenched his fingers around the short gladius that he was carrying, longing to stride across and thrust the point between those grinning jaws, and twist the blade, splintering those fine white teeth. That was one of the men who had murdered his father. Killed him as surely as if they had thrust the sword into his guts.

He looked about fifty, this Gaius Cassius Isidorus. But it was hard to guess. The man brushed his long hair, longer than was the fashion, back over his ears, and Marcus almost smiled. That was why he wore it so long. His ears were small knobs of red flesh. Quite without lobes. Making him look like a runaway slave that had been recaptured and punished by lopping his ears.

There were three more to make the run. One slip on the soft sand and the iron spikes would rip away the side of your head. The Procurator turned from Marcus and went across to join the group by the main gates. Yet again Marcus was aware that he was the subject of their conversation, but he ignored them, concentrating all his attention on the run ahead.

The training had been hard, and the carts came each evening to remove the corpses of those who didn't make it. Mainly the slaves and the prisoners, most of whom were in poor shape. But for someone like Marcus, it wasn't unbearable. The arms training was much as he'd done ever since he could first heft a cut-down sword. The thing he'd found most difficult was mastering the quadriga. The light racing chariot, so different from the war vehicles of his great aunt, the almost legendary Boadicea.

He was next. Unconsciously, his fingers went to his neck to touch the small pebble on its leather thong. An amulet of no obvious value, yet it was above gold for him. It had been given to him by mother's aunt herself. And he still treasured a vague memory of a haughty face, with high cheekbones and eyes that seemed to pierce you through.

"Come on Marcus!" called out the Procurator.

"Come on the traitor's son!" called someone. It was a cry that Marcus had not heard for many months. The time had been when he would have run at the man—he was sure it was Isidorus—and tried to slay him. Now he ignored it, shutting it from the front of his mind. But keeping it locked safely in the room at the back of his brain where revenge festered and swelled like a poisonous worm.

"The whelp's the coward that his traitor father was!" It was said loud enough for every man there to hear.

"Go on, Marcus!" snapped the Procurator, torn between his loyalty to the rich nobles and the knowledge of who Marcus's patron was.

The balls swinging ponderously were easy for him to skip under, watching for the men with the poles. Fending them off with the small buckler on his left arm, and cutting occasionally with the sword in the right.

He had been nearly at the end, with only Ragnar and the skew-faced Thracian to pass.

When the huge open courtyard rang to a shrill scream, and another and another.

Every head turned to the group by the gate, where one of the friends of Isidorus was thrashing around in the sand, kicking up the dust.

Every head but three.

Marcus Julius Britannicus fended off a thrust from Ragnar, grinning through the sweat. Then saw the Thracian, his face seeming frozen with concentration and hatred. Lunging at him. With his blunted spear.

Only it wasn't blunted. The point flicked like the tongue of a snake at him, from the blind side. His right, where he had only the sword to parry. The first blow he cut away, but then one of the iron balls came crushing inward, hissing through the air like an emissary of death. Marcus lowered his head, and the point of the spear darted out again, blooding him on the back of the shoulders.

His eyes sought out the group by the gate, where the man still held everyone's attention, and saw that

51

Isidorus wasn't concerned with his friend. His eyes were locked with Marcus's, and he was smiling.

Off balance, Marcus couldn't dodge the next ball, and it hit his upraised shield, sending him spinning from the walkway, flat on his back. The sword dropping to the sand a dozen paces away. Winded, he looked up at the Thracian, seeing the look of hatred changing to one of triumph.

Time froze, and he knew that he was going to die. The victim of one of the men who had killed his father. And his last thought was of anger and frustration. A rage so bitter that even at that moment of death, it curled his lips, and his mouth filled with the iron taste of defeat.

Marcus thought that he heard the sharp crack of wood snapping, even above the noise of the high-pitched screams, and wondered if it had been the noise of the spear going through his own ribs. Then the light was blotted out and the Thracian loomed above him, the long iron-pointed weapon raised for the final killing blow.

But there had been a third head that hadn't turned.

The Thracian jerked violently, his body lurching toward Marcus, then seeming to hang, like a man floating in water. And he had changed. Before his chest had been a smooth mat of sun-tanned muscles, with only the white stains of old scars to mar it.

Now there was something else.

A red-tipped jagged spike of wood that sprang from the middle of his body, shreds of flesh and grisle hanging from the splintered end. Blood jetted from the gaping wound, splashing all over Marcus, and pattering in the dust around him.

The amazing scene was topped when the body of the Thracian, eyes opened wide in pain and shock, was lifted off its feet and swung sideways, the spear still gripped in its right hand. And flung in a crumpled heap in the dirt.

It had all taken three or four seconds, and in total silence. The Thracian hadn't made a sound, nor had his killer. Who beamed happily at Marcus, reaching down with a hand the size of a smoked ham to help him to his feet. In the background, Marcus was vaguely aware that the screaming was still going on.

"By Odin, Roman! But you have an enemy."

"Nay, Ragnar. I *had* an enemy, and I thank you for your doing."

It had been no mean feat to snap a thick shaft of oak across the knee. And then to lift the corpse clean off its feet. But Ragnar was no ordinary man.

"And what happened after he was dead, my greatest of heroes?"

Marcus had told Agrippina the tale in a different form. Omitting any mention of the part played in it by Isidorus and his friends.

Even as he was being helped up by the massive Northman, he saw the spasm of anger on the face of his father's killer, and saw him kick his friend who thrashed around on the earth. The screaming stopped immediately. And the group disappeared quickly, not even bothering to find out what was causing the commotion at the center of the training ground.

Tiberius Scipius wasn't particularly concerned about the fate of the Thracian. Marcus explained that it had been an accident, and the Procurator didn't bother to look further.

"Shouldn't eat so much undercooked meat, that Antonius. First time I've seen him have a falling fit like that though. Funny business. Thought he'd scream the damned walls down. Still, all over now."

But Marcus noticed that a group had quickly

formed around the corpse. And when they cleared away again, indifferent to one more death among so many, the iron-pointed spear had mysteriously vanished.

The sun was setting as Marcus walked away from the luxurious town house of Flavius Julius Germanicus, husband of the Lady Agrippina. He'd managed to satisfy her five times during the afternoon, and she had clung tearfully to him when he told her that he had to be back at the Ludus before nightfall. In fact he had permission to stay out all night, but Marcus was a believer in moderation. Five times seemed enough for both of them.

And he had promised her that he would call again the next time he was able to leave the strict discipline of the training school.

He had promised Ragnar that he would help the big warrior with simple sword fighting. For all his speed and strength, the albino lacked the skill and polish to fight a straight man-to-man duel with the short Roman swords. Back in his own barren land men fought with axes, or with long blades.

With the shorter gladius, he found that he was constantly misjudging the distance. Hitting inside the opponent, and it was hard for the trainer to teach him to over-reach. To cut and parry and cut again, forcing the other man back with his great power and reach.

The whores were coming out along the streets near to the Via Labicana, smiling at him through their painted lips, flaunting their near-naked bodies through gowns that were so sheer as to be almost transparent. Even had he not come from a tiring bout with Agrippina, he would have refused them. There were too many things that a man could catch from those women, and Marcus valued his health above most things.

Ragnar was already out in the exercise courtyard, cutting and thrusting with a wooden sword at a patient trainer, who kept throwing down his weapon and shouting at the huge man.

"No you heathen bastard! In close! In close!"

But Ragnar stood off and swung the short-bladed gladius as if it were a double-headed war axe. Marcus watched him for a couple of minutes, thinking about the debt of a life that he owed this lonely man, his pale face and hair ghostly in the failing light.

The time would come when he would need to do something about that debt.

FIVE

Metellus Julius Vitrivius and his younger cousin, Lucius Julius Gellius, were both in their late forties. Old enough to have been contemporaries of his father. And yet Condorus was younger. Marcus knew none of the details of the conspiracy that had destroyed his beloved father, but he guessed that Vellius Condorus must have been a beardless youth at the time. Perhaps his part had been to be the messenger.

Scurrying hither and thither like rat behind an arras. Breathing poison into the ears of honest men and closing their minds to truth and honesty.

It was a strange irony that this one man should have been responsible for the deaths of both of Marcus's parents. That thought would make the final revenge so much the sweeter. Marcus yearned each day that passed for the swift arrival of Vellius Condorus and he slept easier at nights knowing that each day brought his most bitter enemy a day closer to him.

Despite all of his efforts to train the Northman, Ragnar still couldn't quite master the Roman sword. But the hours of private practice with Marcus were paying off. He was better. Much better. So much better. So much better that the trainer agreed that he and Marcus should both fight together in the arena in the coming Games.

"Ragnar. Don't lean so far forward when you lunge! One day someone's going to duck under that. And . . . you're very dead."

"All times we must meet that, Marcus, my friend. The blind widowmaker waits for all men all times. And when she calls to us, then all men answer."

Marcus grinned up at him, slapping him on the forearm. "There is no good day to die, you great white-headed ox."

The Northman shook his head. "Not soothly, what you say. Good day to die is in hundredth year with belly full of beer and a bed filled with big-titted virgins."

The Emperor had only called once to Marcus during that month of training. Although the weather was turning colder, they still walked together in the gardens, the guards keeping a dutiful distance. Titus carried a scroll which he read as they walked.

"This is from your Procurator, Marcus. That bean stick of a man. Tiberius Scorpius, is his name?"

"Scipius, my Emperor."

"What?"

"Tiberius Scipius. The Procurator of the Ludus Magnus, my Emperor."

"Quite right. He tells me here of the progress that you have made. He is not the fool he looks, this Procurator."

Marcus waited for the Emperor to go on. He had been aware that he was being studied by Scipius, but this was not unusual. Any potential gladiator who showed real promise never lacked for men to back him. He knew that his skill would carry him through most occasions in the arenas. And he also knew that the giant Ragnar would be an even bigger draw, with his unusual build and even more unusual appearance.

"He compares you to other men he has trained over the last few years. Astacius. Cupido. The black Serpenius. Even mighty Calumorius. I saw him once, just before I went out to win Masada. A wonderful fighter. Looked like a scribe, with little puzzled eyes. Seemed sorry to be in the arena at all, and while his opponent was feeling sorry in turn for this puny little chicken—Swish, and you'd be looking down at your own tripes all covered in sand and flies."

Titus laughed uproariously at the happy memory. Laughter that Marcus managed to join. The names Titus had mentioned were all familiar. One-eyed Argos had told him of the great gladiators of years gone by. Even told him tales of mythical Spartacus.

Spartacus. The slave who escaped. Formed an army. Beat the might of Rome time and time again. Until they sent more men. And still more men. He hid in the crater of Vesuvius from the legions, while his army melted like snow in a spring thaw.

And afterward. Argos had told him how his grandfather had told him how his own father had talked of being taken to see the end of the revolt of Spartacus. Of driving in a cart all the many miles of the Appian Way, from Rome out as far as Capua. And every few paces there was a cross. And on every cross there hung one of the followers of Spartacus.

Six thousand crucifixions.

But they never caught Spartacus himself.

"Do you want to know what Scipius says about you, Marcus Julius Britannicus?"

"Yes, my Emperor."

"Says here you could be better than any of them. Not *are* mind you. But *could* be. I think that the good Procurator is concerned in case you get too large for your sandals. And rightly too. I have seen too many young fools run grinning to embrace Libitina and make their mothers weep. I would not have that happen to you, Marcus."

He laid his hand gently on the younger man's arm, and they stood for a moment in silence. Then Titus moved away, coughing and looking down again at the scroll.

"He records you progress in some detail, in every aspect of the skills of the gladiator. A thorough man, this Scorpius."

"Scipius, my Emperor. His name is Scipius."

There was real anger in the eyes of Titus as he turned toward Marcus, who took a step back, hand falling as it so easily did to the hilt of his sword.

"Marcus, I allowed you to correct me once with no reproach. I here now warned you of it after a second occasion. There will not be a third. Do you understand me?"

"Yes, my Emperor. The name of Scipius is to be Scorpius, and I shall not remind you of such a thing again."

There was a passing moment when he wondered if he had gone too far. History was full of dead men who had thought that they were amusing the Emperor.

But Titus said nothing, pursing his lips. Once more examining the scroll.

"This Scipius, *Scipius*, as I am assured the damned man's name goes. Tells me of swordsmanship. Archery. The driving of chariots. And he mentions a certain Thracian to whom an accident befell. I believe the man is now with his ancestors? Yes? Is there something of that incident that your Emperor should know, Marcus?"

It was a difficult question, and one that he would have to answer quickly.

"There was a distraction during training. One of the onlookers, a friend of Gaius Cassius Isidorus, was taken ill. The Thracian must have been . . . perhaps he was not concentrating on what he was doing. There was nearly an accident and my life was saved by a Northman named Ragnar. That is all there is to tell, my Emperor."

Titus nodded, saying nothing.

"Does Scipius tell you much, my Emperor?"

"Enough to tell me that I have made a good choice with you. He thinks that you will be ready for a first appearance in the Games in three days. You and this Northman will fight with the retiarii against the murmillones. Scipius," he paused for a moment, "Scipius claims that your best skills at present will be shown with the net and trident against the sword and shield."

"And Ragnar also?"

"Aye, Marcus. And this white-face man from the snows. Is he your friend?"

"I owe him my life."

"Then you think he is." Titus sighed, shaking his head. "Marcus, listen to my words. To be a successful fighter for the crowds is like being the Emperor of all Rome. You can afford no friends. And no enemies."

"No enemies, my Emperor?"

"Alive."

"But Ragnar is honest and true. I know this, my Emperor, and I have had cause to know and mistrust many men."

"In the arena, Marcus, there will come a time, be it

sooner or later, when you will have to make a choice. Between a friend, and life."

Two evenings later, the training school held the great supper for the gladiators who would be fighting on the morrow. It would be in a small Amphitheater, to aid the election of some official. None of the men knew who he was, nor cared. But he was putting up some handsome purses of gold for the winners.

And the losers would never worry anyway.

The cena libera, this great banquet, was enjoyed by many of the older hands at the game, but dreaded by most of the new men. The food was excellent, provided by tomorrow's Editor, and the wine flowed like a winter stream. To his surprise, Marcus noticed that many of the scarred veterans drank their wine neat, instead of diluting it like most people did.

The cream of Roman society came to these meals, enjoying the thrill of sharing the moment with these men, knowing that at least a third of them would not live to see the sun set on the next day.

Among them was Gaius Cassius Isidorus, surrounded by the usual throng of giggling sycophants and ladies of the streets. Marcus spotted him as soon as he came in, and nudged Ragnar at his elbow.

He had avoided telling the Northman of the reasons behind his hatred of Isidorus, merely mentioning that there was a feud between their families. A concept that Ragnar found easy to understand.

Some of the poor wretches, incompetent with weapons, knew that this would be their last meal, and yet they ate nothing. Stomachs and throats dry and frozen with fear. They tugged at the togas of the visitors, begging them to take last messages from the Ludus to their loved ones outside. One young boy, whose father had been ruined by a money lender, kept weeping, filling up his mug with wine, and draining it in one gulp. And filling it again. And again.

Marcus had tried to check him, knowing that to drink that way meant certain death in the morning, but the boy had shrugged off his advice, utterly lost in his misery and despair.

Isidorus strolled around the ranks of tables, picking up a bite here and there, and patting some gladiators that he knew on the shoulder, with a jest for some. The Procurator was with him, his eyes flicking to Marcus, and then looking embarrassedly away again.

At last the group reached the table where Marcus sat silently eating with Ragnar and a few other men. The tension between the two somehow communicated itself to the others, and there was a well of silence amid the hubbub.

"Well, well, my brothers. What do we have here? I find a somewhat unpleasant odor, Procurator. Perhaps there is something going rotten here. Like a coward whose father was also a coward. I find the stench of cowardice an offense to my nostrils."

Marcus laid down the cup of wine, resting the flat of his hands on the rough wooden table, slowly levering himself to his feet, turning until he was looking Isidorus full in the face. The noble smiled cynically at him, knowing that if the young man made a false move he could have him butchered on the spot.

"Yes? Have you something to say to me you baseborn whoreson?"

"You are Gaius Cassius Isidorus, are you not? My father told me of you."

"And what did your traitor father tell you of me? Only good I trust?"

Marcus smiled at him, watching the man's eyes. Seeing them twitch uncertainly. This wasn't the way that Isidorus had thought things would go. And he was becoming uncertain.

"He told me that you were a man who attracted many friends."

"That's true, is it not?" There was a chorus of agreement from the crowd around him. But the tone was unsure. Puzzled. They had come to see this impudent gladiator lose his temper with Gaius Cassius, so that he could be executed on the spot for striking a noble. And somehow, it wasn't working out that way. The calm young man with the broad shoulders and deep brown eyes simply smiled at the insults.

"Many friends," he said.

"True."

"The very best that your money could buy you."

"Why you . . . !"

But Marcus had turned his back on him, sitting down at the table with a calmness he didn't feel, picking up his wine again. Winking at Ragnar, who sat stiffly across from him, one hand out of sight in his lap.

"Procurator! Have that man flogged!" spluttered the raging Isidorus.

"He is a free man and a citizen. His father was nobly born. I'm sorry. He did not strike you?"

"Yes. No. No, he did not."

He saw how Marcus had caught him in his own trap, and had beaten him. Just as Marcus would not dare to strike him, so he dare not strike Marcus. Had he been a slave . . . But he wasn't. So all he could do was bluster and shout, while Marcus sat and ate, and others turned to watch the curious spectacle.

At last his friends urged him away, but he paused and leaned over the younger man, his breath rank in Marcus's nostrils.

"I shall not forget this. I shall see that you die."

As he stalked away, Marcus called after him. "We shall all die. But let it not concern you, Gaius Cassius Isidorus. I shall be there to make sure that all your funeral arrangements are such as befit a man like you."

There was a ripple of laughter and the rich man stormed out, leaving the big double doors wide open. After the moment had passed and the talk resumed around the tables, Ragnar slowly pulled his hand from his lap. Holding a long slim-bladed knife. Grinning at Marcus as he tucked it into his belt.

"If you had died there, he would have lived for only a heartbeat longer," he said.

Marcus reached across the table and they clenched hands. Both feeling the growing friendship.

The Amphitheater was only half-full. The weather was cold and miserable, and the Editor had been unable to get any of the top names to fight for him. He'd been prepared to lay out a hundred aurei to get Atascadorus to fight for him, but the black had recently been awarded the rudis of freedom for the third time and was still drinking his success away.

Rain threatened, and the Procurator had actually been to see the Editor that morning early to ask him whether he would be prepared to postpone the Games to a more auspicious day. But the elections were too close for that, so the trumpets blared and forty pairs of gladiators marched out to salute the man with their swords.

Marcus and Ragnar were both to fight with the net and trident, although the Northman had shown little enthusiasm for the weapons. And less skill with them.

Marcus had mastered them early, when he had fought around the water meadows of their home in Britain, with a long ash stake for his trident and a square of material torn from one of his old togas, weighted at the edges with pebbles for the net. And Argos hopped around, dodging his clumsy casts, prodding him with a blunted practice gladius.

"Poor bloody turn out," muttered the man on Marcus's right hand. "Surprised to see so many of the quality here. Don't usually bother with this sort of thing so late in the year."

Marcus looked around, glancing at the expensive boxes near the front of the arena. Not surprised to see that Isidorus was there, lolling back wrapped in a heavy woolen cloak.

And, Marcus saw with a thrill of pleasure that fired his blood, at his side were two other men he had cause to welcome. The cousins, Metellus Julius Vitruvius and Lucius Julius Gellius. A triumvirate of killers, come to watch him. Something must have alarmed them about a possible danger from the son of Lucian Julius Britannicus. Maybe the favor of the Emperor toward Marcus had warned them.

Now they had come to see him.

To see him fight.

To see him die?

The handle of the trident felt cold and slick to his fingers, and as they marched out again, feet sliding through the damp sand, Marcus wondered who the Gods would pit him against. As long as it wasn't Ragnar, he didn't mind.

There were few men fighting as murmillones that he feared. Though there was one man he wasn't sure of. He'd only appeared at the Ludus a day earlier, and the Procurator had left him alone. Older than most. Probably past twenty-five, with massive thigh muscles and a heavy body showing the first signs of running to fat. He was called Trebonius.

The Procurator was standing just inside the main gate to the arena, and he held the bag with the lot numbers in it. Marcus was near the front and drew twenty-four, showing it to Scipius and dropping it in the discard box on the floor.

Ragnar was drawn against another notice and he walked over to join Marcus. "Who are you with, brother?"

"I don't know. I don't think that twenty-three has been drawn yet."

"Oh."

"What does that mean, my tiny brother?"

Ragnar didn't smile at the jest. "It means danger for you. Take care. I saw this Trebonius draw a number, and show it to no man but Scipius. Then he took it and slipped it into a purse. Not in the box with others. That number was twenty-three. Beware."

"I thank you, brother Ragnar. But it is no surprise. I see who sits and watches. They have not come to cheer me on my way. But I am surprised that Scipius is a party to this. He is a fool."

It was a dull day with dull combats, and the crowd was beginning to get restive. The Editor had tried sending out young boys to shower them with presents from slingshots but several of the boys began to brawl and the whole thing ended in an unseemly squabble and a burst of jeering.

Scipius came down from the stands to tell them that they were to fight better and harder, and that it wasn't likely that any of them would be given quarter. The small crowd wasn't in that sort of mood.

He'd been keeping Ragnar up his sleeve as a special attraction, but now was the time that the mob needed some kind of extra diversion. And so in went the Northman, with a quick hand clasp from Marcus. As soon as they'd gone, the Procurator turned to where Marcus stood, carefully folding his net.

"You next, Britannicus."

"Scipius" called Marcus in a soft voice.

"What?" the tall skinny man turned and stood near to him, against an angle of the wall.

"A man who runs with the wolves, may find that he falls victim to the bear."

Scipius went as pale as a sheet, and for a moment seemed as though he was going to fall. "What? I don't know what you mean, I don't . . ."

Marcus shook his head. "Then all is well. But if you do know . . ." He let the sentence hang unfinished in the air like the threat of a naked blade.

The appearance of the giant Northman, who had totally refused to fight in the heavy arm protector of the retiarius, was the signal for the day to improve. A watery sun managed to squeeze its way through the overhanging clouds, and the mob began to brighten up with it.

This great man, with his totally white body and swishing mane of silver hair was something to talk about, and they began to cheer and stamp, their earlier ill-humor forgotten in the way common to all crowds at Games.

The man who was to fight with him, wearing the enveloping helmet of the murmillo, clutching the short stabbing sword in a trembling hand, was less well received. Ragnar had won a fearsome reputation in the Ludus, and the novice was clearly terrified.

"Fetch a ladder so you can reach him!" bellowed one of the arena wits at the boy.

The Editor gave the signal for them to fight, leaning forward in his seat, clearly pleased that things were looking up for him. Perhaps the vast amount of money it cost to stage a Games was not going to be wasted.

Ragnar didn't disappoint the crowd, though there were some who would have rather seen him take a little longer with his victory.

He swung the net around his head in a hissing arc of death, the small lead weights giving it a fearful momentum, and advanced on the other novice, holding the long trident by its middle as though it were only a light cane. The boy backed away from him, making feeble passes at him with his shield. When the net hit the small buckler, it wrenched it clean out of his hand, leaving him with only the sword.

"He's dead, the stupid bastard," muttered Trebonius, standing unexpectedly at Marcus's elbow, peering through the iron grille of the gates.

The mysterious gladiator was calmer than any of them, casually picking his nose as he waited his turn, his helmet sitting on the floor by his feet. Marcus looked sideways at him, wondering who he really was and where Isidorus had found him.

"You've fought here before?" asked Marcus.

"Dozens of times, boy. No. Make that hundreds."

"Then why don't I know your name?" asked Marcus curiously. "I've heard of most of the top men, and never of Trebonius."

"Listen to me, Marcus whatever your name is. I've been paid to come here and do a job for . . . someone. Someone who doesn't like you, and that's a fact. I don't know you. Don't dislike you, though I reckon you're one of those bloody patricians. You might as well know it, as you'll be dead in a minute or two, and no way out."

Marcus nodded. "Trebonius isn't your real name?"

"That's right, boy. And I fear you won't even have time to know what it is, because there's your big friend there finishing that poor fish, and we're in next. Come on and I'll make it fast."

Ragnar had followed up the boy in the middle of the arena with a look of such dreadful violence on his face that the wretched youth had tripped over his own feet, dropping his sword. In such a case the gladiator who was in the position to win was supposed to hold off and wait for the signal from the Editor.

The Northman had no time for such niceties of convention. He simply hefted the trident, dropping the net to one side, and rammed it clean through the wriggling boy, under the breastbone, leaving him kicking and screaming, pinned to the sand of the arena, blood pouring from his mouth and nostrils.

The crowd cheered wildly as the giant stalked away, never once turning back either to look at his victim, or to acknowledge the shouts.

An assistant wearing the cloak and disguise of Hermes Psychopompos scampered across the sand, clutching the iron hammer of his trade. Knelt beside the boy and struck him a savage blow across the temple. The legs thrashed and kicked like a slingshot rabbit, and then he was still.

It took three men to remove the trident, so powerful had been the death blow from Ragnar.

"Now us. Remember what I said. Just let me get in close and I'll make it quick and easy."

Marcus followed Trebonius through the gate, not having a chance to speak to Ragnar, across the sand. Feeling it again, testing it for grip. Looking up at the weak sun to get his bearings straight. He waited until they were standing side by side at the center of the arena, and ready for the sign to begin the fight before he spoke to the burly gladiator who had been, he now knew, hired to kill him.

"Trebonius," he hissed.

"What?"

"I once saw your mother on the Via Cloaca making love to a donkey."

"What?" Trebonius's voice echoed in the bronze cavern of his helmet.

"The Greek way. And I threw her a handful of quadrantes. More than the slut was worth."

It may have been words, but it sounded more like an inarticulate bellow of sheer rage. Without waiting for the signal, Trebonius slashed sideways at Marcus, intending to strike his head from his body. But Marcus was no longer standing there.

"Shame!" roared a hundred voices, seeing the foul trick that the murmillo had tried to play.

But Marcus grinned, balancing lightly on the balls of his feet, the net hanging easily across his right arm, connected to his wrist by a length of strong cord. The gladius weaving a pattern of death in his left hand.

"She picked them from the floor in her . . ."

He never had time to finish the sentence, with its obscene lie, before Trebonius, blind anger making him forget all his skill, rushed in at him, sword jabbing for the eyes of his persecutor.

"Too slow, old man," he taunted Trebonius as he skipped out of the way of the mad charge.

While the heavier man was still turning, Marcus tried a cast with the net, narrowly missing Trebonius's feet. He quickly tugged it back, trotting away while he adjusted its folds once more.

Trebonius came charging after him, breath rasping in his chest. And Marcus ran from him. Not too fast to make him lose patience. Just fast enough to encourage him to keep after him.

"Get the wings off your heels!" called someone from the upper rows.

Marcus looked around at the shout, seeming startled

by it. And appeared to trip on his face, landing in a sprawl of limbs. A woman screamed near the box of the Editor, and a man's voice, familiar in its sneer, called out: "Finish the dog!"

Trebonius was only too eager to obey the voice of his master.

Too eager.

Much too eager.

As he paused over the prostrated and helpless figure of Marcus, he was unable to resist the temptation to check the death stroke and look around to the Editor for the formality of permission to slaughter the defeated man.

Which was when Marcus made his move. He had been watching the murmillo from under his shaded arm, ready to roll if he hadn't checked his blow. When he did, Marcus pushed hard with his hands, kicking up and back with both feet like a fly-maddened horse.

His metal-tipped sandals hit the gladiator in the pit of the stomach, below the armored kilt that was worn to protect his genitals. Which was quite useless against a blow from beneath.

Marcus felt the blow jar through his feet and rolled back like an acrobat, coming up on his feet, the net ready and the sword extended.

Trebonius had sunk to his knees and was vomiting up his breakfast, retching the sour lees of last night's wine, his sword and shield in the sand, the yellow strings of puke dribbling out of the bottom of the all-enveloping helmet, with its sporting fish in bright silver a'top it.

The crowd had fallen suddenly silent, then there was a roar of approval as they realized the cunning of the trick that had enabled Marcus to beat Trebonius. The older man still crouched on his hands and knees, coughing and heaving, hunched over in the dirt. Helpless.

Marcus slipped the knot off the net and transferred the keen-edged gladius to his right hand, stepping in closer to the stricken man. Watching even now, in case Trebonius was faking and might spring up at him. But he doubted it.

A raucous voice bellowed from the very highest and cheapest tier of seats. "He's as tricky as a fox, that one."

"Yes! Vulpus the fox."

"Vulpus! Vulpus the fox!!"

Around the arena the cry was picked up and repeated, rising into the thin winter air, echoing back and forth, as the crowd recognized the arrival of a possible new hero in the arena.

Marcus looked up at Isidorus, but his box was empty. Turned to the Editor, who was standing up, amazed by the rapid reversal of fortune.

Trebonius tried desperately to control his breathing, fingers fumbling at the straps of his helmet, finally managing to remove it and drop it in the vomit-sodden sand at his feet. Turning his head to appeal to the crowd, feebly raising one hand. Never once looking up at the victor, poised over him like a butcher before a sacrificial calf.

No one shouted for freedom and life. The Amphitheater rebounded with cries of: "Iugula! Iugula!! Iugula!" directed at the box of the Editor. It would have been a foolish man who ignored such an outcry, and the politician looked down into the arena and calmly turned down his thumb in the universal gesture of doom.

"Good old Vulpus! Stick him, Vulpus!" called out a voice.

Trebonius, or whatever his name was, looked up at

72

Marcus, squinting into the sun. And his eyes were the eyes of an old, old man. Who saw with the clarity of crystal that he had lived too long. Marcus had seen it before in the arena, when the older man fell to a younger.

"The cup passes," he said, his voice barely carrying to the kneeling man.

"Aye. Strike true as I would have done for you," replied Trebonius, bowing his head.

For a man with such massive muscles, his neck parted before the sweep of the gladius with surprising ease, the head dropping to the sand with a dull, wet thud, to roll a little, the blood and vomit and dirt matting in the cropped hair.

A bright fountain spurted into the air, the light wind catching it and blowing it into fine spray, dappling the arena floor with crimson, and the body toppled slowly forward and lay still.

Marcus turned away from the corpse, and raised his sword in tribute to the Editor and to the crowd, its blade slick with blood. Moved around slowly, saluting each segment of the spectators, his only regret that Isidorus and his murderous friends had not stayed to see the last act of their little play end in such a way.

The cheering burst about his ears, crashing like the breaking surf on the rocky coast of Britain, and Marcus stood erect before it, feeling a fierce pride and swell of exultation. He had fought and won, and the crowd loved him for it.

"Vulpus!"

"Vulpus!!"

"Vulpus!!!"

SIX

"A plague?"

"Aye. It sweeps across Gaul from the east."

"It will never reach Rome, my Emperor."

Titus shook his head. He and Marcus walked together, muffled up against the cold spell that enveloped the Imperial City. Word of the first major appearance of his gladiator had sped to the ears of Titus, and he was pleased. The more popular a fighter was, the more likely he was to have a familiar name, donated by the upper seats of the Amphitheater.

"Vulpus. The Fox. It likes me well, Marcus. In four or five days there will be another Games. I shall be there. I would like you to fight again, but against someone less dangerous than this Trebonius."

"Did your agents find out his real name?"

"No. That is one secret that will die with him. But you are sure that Scipius is involved?"

Marcus nodded. The lean Procurator had avoided him since the incident, leaving the training to others.

Titus shook his head again. "That man is a fool, after all. I would rather have men about me that are less lean. There was always something about him that . . . but let it pass. There are more important things for us to talk on."

A bitter wind blew down from the east bringing the bitter taste of approaching winter with it. The guards at the palace wore their cloaks of scarlet, and stamped their feet as they marched to try and keep warm.

The Emperor rubbed his hands together, his breath clouding in front of his face as he spoke. "That Northman may prove his mettle again. Atascadorus has sobered enough again to realize that he needs more gold so that he can go and drink and wench again. I shall match them together. Sword against trident. It will please the crowd."

"I fear that Ragnar will be hard pressed to win. He's the strongest, fastest man I've ever seen. But he lacks skill and experience. Someone like Atascadorus could cut him to shreds of bloody flesh."

"I shall be there, Marcus. If that happens, then I may be able to show mercy and spare him for another day."

Marcus coughed. "This cold . . . But Ragnar is not one who will ever know when he is beaten. Twice in mock combat at the Ludus he has gone wild in the fighting. His eyes seem to turn inward and look into the depths of his own mind. It took five men to hold him down after one victory. Froth dappled his lips and his tongue bled where he had bitten it in his blind anger."

"They say that is how this sickness takes men. First a great fever that burns and blazes. Then swellings in

75

the groin and under the arms that grow monstrously and turn black and then burst with foul humors. Few that it touches live to see a seventh dawn."

"Vellius Condorus comes through Gaul?"

"Aye, Marcus. But he will be here in Rome within the week. And then . . ." There was a silence between the two men. "What progress against your enemies? I hear of their plots against you. What of yours against them?"

"I cannot conspire, my Emperor. I must wait my chance. Then strike."

"My agents tell me that these men also plot against . . . but that is not truly your concern. I hear that Isidorus is to visit the building of the new Flavian Amphitheater tomorrow. It would be well if there was a man there who knew a little of the needs of the arena."

"Someone, my Emperor?"

"Someone like you, Vulpus. Someone very much like you."

After the massive Amphitheater of Taurus had been destroyed in the great fire of Rome, Vespasian had begun the building of an arena that would dwarf anything that had gone before. The site was perfect. Between the Caelius, the Esquiline and the Velia, not far from the colossus of the sun within the Golden House. Ironically, one of the favorite fishponds of Nero had to be filled in for the new and spectacular Amphitheater.

The stone was light-colored travertine limestone, carried to Rome from the quarries of Albulae near Tibur.

Now, after twelve years abuilding, it was very nearly complete, and all the signs were that it might be opened within the next few months.

Oval in shape, it would take a man over five hundred paces to walk clear around it, and it towered up a good spear-cast into the sky. Sixty paces up, so one of the builders had told Marcus. Four layers high, each succeeding layer in a different style.

But Marcus wasn't interested in the seats. Who would own the marble boxes and how many could sit here or there. Nor how they would get in and out. Not even with the arrangements for keeping them cool and supplied with food and drink during the long hot days. He was only interested in the size and shape of the arena, and the way things were laid out below the sand. The cages and rooms that honeycombed the lower layers of the vast building.

The weather was dull and rainy when he went along to carry out the orders of Titus and inspect the progress of the great Amphitheater of Flavius. The men who spidered across the web of trembling wooden scaffolding, putting some of the finishing touches to the upper levels, worked with more care than usual. It would be too easy for freezing fingers to betray you and let you plunge down to your death in the area below of what would be the actual arena.

It had become one of the sights of the city, and Marcus was delighted to have a day free from the Ludus to go and inspect it all for himself. He wore a short woollen tunic, and had taken the precaution of wrapping himself in a heavy cloak, that the drizzling rain was making heavier by the minute. He had been surprised at how easily he had been allowed to slip away, as discipline in the training school was usually so strict.

Perhaps it had something to do with the nonappearance of the Procurator. For the first time since Marcus had begun the rigorous training, the lean figure of Scipius had been absent from the first meal of the day, and a message had come down to the gladiators that he had fallen ill and was likely to be ill for some time. If he recovered at all.

"Something he ate," commented one of the older men.

"Someone who paid him for a little extra work on the side. And maybe someone else came to hear of it," Marcus whispered to Ragnar, who now always sat at his elbow.

Poison was traditionally one of the strongest weapons of an Emperor for dealing with those who went against him.

Marcus walked along the colonnade, toward the underground chambers where the animals would be caged as soon as the arena was opened. As he walked slowly along one of the sloping corridors, he heard voices ahead of him.

"Go and tell Sextus where I am and that I'll be out in a very short time. And be quick about it or I'll have you flogged."

The voice was the cold sneer of Gaius Cassius Isidorus.

Marcus pulled back into the shadows, listening to the noise of feet pattering up toward him. The slave of Isidorus scampering to do his master's bidding.

He had no chance, feeling only an arm like a band of iron that clamped across his windpipe, while a hard hand over his mouth shut off any cry. The dimness of the tunnel gave way to total darkness, and the last sound that Sextus heard was a great roaring in his ears.

Marcus gently laid the body down, dragging it by the shoulders into a smaller side passage, where it might go for days without being discovered. The work below ground was nearly finished, and the workmen were all concentrated out in the open, trying to get as much completed as possible before winter closed in on them.

Drawing his sword from its soft leather sheath, Marcus began to walk quietly down the slope, feeling carefully with his sandaled feet in case there were any stones left across the passage that might betray him. But it was clear.

"This will be for some of the beasts?"

"Aye. Though they would do well to make it for the Nazarenes. They are the greatest animals from what I hear of them."

Two! Isidorus, and another. Not a voice he recognized. But a man who would need to die if Marcus was to reach the man he wanted. Just as the slave, Sextus had paid the price for working for a master like Isidorus. Marcus felt no pang of compunction toward the unlucky wretch. He would have slain even his dearest friend if it would have helped him toward his ultimate revenge.

His sight gradually became easier as he got used to the dimness. An occasional torch flared and guttered in the drafts that whispered about him, but their pools of light ended in great swathes of deeper blackness.

The corridor opened out into a larger area, and the light was better. Marcus saw a barred grille on the far side that he guessed must lead to some form of lifting arrangement to get animals and men to the surface of the arena as quickly as possible.

Only two men stood there in that open space. Both with their backs to him. The floor was dotted with great hunks of stone, some ready carved, and some rough and cracked, waiting for the slaves to come and clean them out at some later date. In the center of the chamber, near where the two men stood, was what looked like a large pit of some kind. But how large and how deep, it was impossible for Marcus to see.

With so much loose stone about, it was difficult for Marcus to get close enough to take them both, and the room was far enough below ground for none of the noises of the men working above to penetrate.

Isidorus and his friend had their heads together, talking quietly, and Marcus wondered what plots they laid in that dark, secret place.

Trying to use the patches of shadow as cover, he began to make his way toward the men, but his luck was out. When he was still a good twenty paces from them, they both turned, and started toward him. It was then that he realized what a great advantage lay with him. He had his back to the lights, and so could only be seen in silhouette. While they were fully in the light.

The glow from the torches was good enough for Marcus to recognize that head of Isidorus, the hair a little too long to hide the malformed ears. He didn't recognize the other man, who also wore a long cloak against the biting cold. They glanced up at him as they moved closer, and he saw with a thrill that neither knew him in the gloom.

"I swear that he is not the man that his brother was," said Isidorus as they approached. And Marcus wondered who they discussed in that way. Perhaps it was an innocent conversation. And perhaps it was not.

The friend of Isidorus was on his side as they passed by him, and Marcus hid his sword under his cloak, pretending to slip, and fall against the other man. Throwing his left arm around his neck, and thrusting and twisting the keen blade of his sword into his heart. He felt the sour exhalation of pain and shock, the warm blood trickling out over the hilt, sticky on his fingers.

The killing was so swift and clean that the man

never cried out, merely slumping in Marcus's arms like a marionette with its strings all cut.

"Damn your clumsiness!" barked Isidorus, seeing the stranger falling, and seeming to drag down his friend. "Are you well, Publius?"

Marcus let the corpse lie on the damp rocks, and stood up, facing the first of the men who had been responsible for the bitter death of his father.

"Publius sleeps, as soon you will sleep, you foresworn cur!"

"Marcus Julius Britannicus! Ho, Sextus! To your master! Treachery!"

Marcus smiled, taking a step closer to Isidorus, who backed away from him, toward the pit that gaped in the rubble-littered floor.

"Call your slave, Isidorus! He too sleeps and will not waken to your call."

"Help! Murder! Help! Help!"

The cries of the desperate man echoed around and around, seeming to mock Isidorus. But the chamber was so far underground, and the men above so far away, that there was little chance of any aid.

"You are afraid, are you not. My father feared nothing that walked on this earth. It was only four crawling serpents that brought him low. Serpents that weaved themselves about him and trapped him, so that he could find no way out, and so fell on his sword."

"It was not my idea. It was the others."

"Aye," said Marcus, mockingly. "Vitruvius, Gellius and the foul Condorus. They held a blade to your neck and made you lie and lie and lie again."

Isidorus continued to back away from the advancing figure, until his heel caught on the brink of the hole, dislodging a shower of earth and pebbles. Marcus heard them rattle down with a grim smile of satisfaction. The pit was deep enough for his purposes.

81

In the dim light it was possible to see the face of his enemy working away nervously, his hands knotting and tangling in the hem of his splendid cloak. "Please. If it be money, then you shall have gold beyond your dreams. Or if you wish me to leave Rome, then I shall go. Abjure everything and retire to live out the rest of the days in quiet in the country."

Marcus laughed, genuinely amused by Isidorus's frantic babble. "You think I will let you live. You scum! None of you are fit to lace up my father's sandals, and yet he died through you. Give me your sword!"

"Why?"

"Because if you do not, then I shall cut you down and take it from you. Quickly you lop-eared dog!"

Almost in tears, the noble reached under his cloak, and drew his sword, throwing it on the ground in front of Marcus, its blade sending up a tinkling shower of sparks.

"Now, we shall settle a long debt, my lord Isidorous. It has many years in the balance."

Holding his own sword out, point flicking at the man's throat, he advanced in a shuffling rush. Isidorus gave a shriek like a scalded woman and took three steps back. And screamed again.

For the last step was on thin air, sending him toppling backward out of sight, to land with a crash in the pit. Marcus clearly heard the crack of bone and walked cautiously forward, hoping that the fall hadn't killed Isidorus, giving him a quick, clean death.

Groaning from the darkness told him that the man still lived, and he quickly picked a burning torch from its sconce. Holding it in his left hand as he stood balanced on the edge of the drop, so that its smoky glow lit up the bottom of the hole.

Isidorus lay awkwardly in one corner of the pit,

holding his right ankle, his toga and cloak bundled up over his legs. Moaning with pain. "My leg is broken, you damnable swine! Go for help before I die of the agony."

To his amazement, Marcus realized that the man didn't realize that he was truly about to die. He somehow thought that this would be the extent of Marcus's revenge for his father's death.

The young man stepped back from the edge, picking up the discarded sword of Isidorus, his own blade now safely back in its sheath. It was more of a child's toy than a real weapon. Modeled on the gladius of the Legions, but with a thin blade, chased in silver, the hilt a mass of precius stones set in carved bone.

He returned to the pit and dropped the sword in, taking care that it fell close to the hand of the injured man. It clanged in the darkness, and Isidorus looked at it in bewilderment.

"Have your senses left you, Britannicus? Firstly you take my sword, and now you give it me back. Is it because I can no longer harm you with it?"

"You will harm only one more person before you die," said Marcus.

"Why? I don't understand you. Oh, curse this damned leg!"

"You. You will take that sword and ram it into your own guts."

"What?"

"The harder the better. Isidorus. I am told that it only pains worse if you are faint-hearted in the thrust."

There was no reply, and Marcus wondered if the man had fainted away. He leaned over a little further, the torch smoking in his eyes. He saw that Isidorus had managed to half stand, pulling himself up the wall of the chamber. He held his dainty sword in his right hand, looking at it with a wondering expression as though he'd never seen it before.

For a moment Marcus thought that he might be thinking of cutting up at his legs, but the pit was too deep for that.

"I cannot do it." The voice was flat and without emotion. "And you cannot make me. If you go now and leave me, then perhaps you might live. You have been too clever for yourself, as I cannot get out. But neither can you get in."

It was true. But Marcus was prepared for Isidorus to refuse to stick himself. He would need some incentive. He stooped and picked up a sharp-edged hunk of white stone, chipped from the corner of a larger block.

Took careful aim and threw it, not too hard, at the crippled man, hitting him a jarring blow on the arm, making him drop his sword and cry out.

"Pick it up," said Marcus softly, his voice as cold as death.

"No! Damn you!"

As a boy back in misty Britain, Marcus had often roamed the fields with his sling and a pouch filled with pebbles. But he had also been skilled at throwing stones, using a smooth underarm flick, cutting back with the wrist to give the missile greater impetus. To a man who had once been able to bring down a scampering rabbit, it was unfairly easy to pick out where he wanted to hit Isidorus, trapped and helpless in the black hole.

The older man tried to shield himself from the stones by wrapping his head and shoulders in the thick cloak, tugging up his toga. But that left his skinny legs white and bare.

The second stone hit him on the knee, the third

higher up on the thigh, only a finger span from the white linen drawers.

Isidorus rolled around, like a broken-backed beetle, his voice shrill with the continuing pain.

"No! I beg you! Help me! Sextus! Publius! Aid me and you shall have everything I own. Let me live. Aaaargh! You bastard filth! Please stop!"

Time was passing, and there was always the chance that someone might be walking in that area, and hear the noise.

There were stones of all sizes about and Marcus heaved up one the size of a man's head, holding it in both hands, straining with it to the edge of the pit, judging the position of Isidorus in the blackness by his whimperings. Hoping it wouldn't crush his skull. Letting it go.

Hearing the crunch as it hit home on flesh, and the cry of agony, with a new note of despair.

"Use your sword as did my father."

"No!"

More smaller stones, aimed now mainly at Isidorus's face and head. One hitting him just above the eye, covering his face in a sheet of bright blood. Another cracking into the noble's jaw, leaving him to spit out broken teeth in a welter of bloody spittle.

"The sword, Isidorus. Though you have lived like a cur in the gutters of Rome, yet you may die like a man."

The silence was only broken by his sobbing, the noise reverberating around the great underground room. The torch was nearly spent, but still gave Marcus enough light to see the appalling condition of Gaius Cassius Isidorus.

The large stone had broken one shoulder, giving him a crook-backed, deformed appearance, half-lying and half-kneeling in one corner, now making no attempt to protect himself from the hail of stones. His toga was soaked through with blood, running from a dozen cuts. He turned his face up to the guttering light, one eye closed beneath a purple bruise, his mouth hanging open as he panted for breath through mouthfuls of crimson.

"Spare me," he said, his voice so weak that Marcus could scarcely hear him.

"The sword," he repeated remorselessly. "Take your sword and make an end of it."

There was no answer.

It took a half-dozen more of the sharp-edged stones, thrown with increasing violence, before Isidorus spoke again.

"No more."

"Then do it."

"No more . . ."

Marcus waved his hand to clear away the pall of smoke from the dying light, staring down into the square hole, at where his enemy struggled like a landed fish, threshing around in his own blood as he reached for the hilt of his sword, trying to pick it up with slick fingers.

"My arm is broken . . ."

"Then rest the hilt against the floor and fall on it, you foul wretch."

There was not the least sign of pity in Marcus's voice, seeing the man trying to kill himself. Remembering the way they had tried to stop him from seeing his father's corpse, the unadorned hilt of his cavalry sword still protruding from his stomach, his fingers still gripping it.

Isidorus managed to place the sword point up, kneeling over it. "Commend me to my friends," he mumbled through broken lips.

"I shall send them to join you, Gaius Cassius Isidorus."

"Farewell," said the noble toppling on the sword. Which was so heavily ornamented that it failed to penetrate properly and bent after it had entered his skin, angling up toward his liver, missing the heart and lungs. Blood jetted out from the slit, and he cried out.

"I cannot."

"Again," said Marcus ruthlessly. "Withdraw it and strike again."

Twice more Isidorus groveled in a spreading pool of blood, hacking at himself with the twisted blade. Marcus could see the yellow loops of intestine protruding through one of the deeper cuts, but still the man didn't die. Finally he fell sideways, the dying torch reflected off the jewels in the white hilt, still rammed into his stomach. Still moving feebly, but too weak to end himself.

At the last Marcus was moved, more by repulsion than by any sentiment for the mewling broken creature that writhed at the bottom of the black pit, and dropped the torch, picking up another massive block of stone, fully as heavy as a grown man. Bracing his legs he staggered with it, holding it by the corners, feeling the rough edges digging into his fingers.

And dropped it.

There was a dreadful splintering sound, and then silence.

Marcus followed that up with a dozen more of the large boulders, hearing them grind against each other as they fell into the darkness. Before leaving he threw in a number of slightly smaller stones, taking another torch from the wall to look down in the hole. Seeing that nothing remained visible of Isidorus. Just a tangled jumble of cracked stones.

When he walked out again into the fresh air, it was beginning to rain.

"He said nothing more before he died?"

"No, my Emperor."

"No mention of myself? Or of any form of plot with any others?"

"No, my Emperor."

Titus walked across the mosaic floor to look out along the long corridor toward the main courtyard of the palace. "Then it was well done, Marcus. I praise you for it. Now there are three others."

"Yes. But I have begun. I have heard of the words of the Nazarenes. They too, my Emperor, would be pleased."

"Why?"

"For I have begun by casting the first stone."

SEVEN

Vellius Condorus was in Rome!

He had arrived the day before the Games that Titus was giving. The last before winter shut the arenas, and one of the most splendid of the year. And Condorus would be there.

Already he had tried to see Titus, but the Emperor was careful to avoid him, not wishing to be implicated in any way in whatever Marcus might be planning.

But his star gladiator was not yet ready. After the killing of Isidorus he was prepared to lie low for a while, knowing that the other conspirators would suspect that it had been his hand behind the butchery.

The only word that Titus had sent him through a trusted agent was that the subprocurator was unwell. A cold he thought that he had picked up traveling with such loyal speed to get to Rome to answer the summons of his beloved Emperor. But it was not likely to keep him from the arena on the morrow.

Marcus was glad of that.

"Remember. If he comes in close, then try and keep him off with the trident. Understand, Ragnar?"

The pale lips drew back in a smile. The tall Northman tossed back his glittering mane of white hair, patting his friend on the arm. "Worry not for me, my little brother. When the Widowmaker calls, then she may find that I do not hear her."

Marcus grinned back. He knew as well as any of the trainers in the Ludus that Ragnar was one of those great natural fighters, and only today would they find out whether a man like him could hope to beat one of the greatest of the technical gladiators. The mighty black, Atascadorus.

There had been a buzz of rumor all over the city at the news of this combat. And he had been pleased to hear that there was also talk of himself among the alleys and wine shops. Of the cunning young Marcus Julius Britannicus. Nicknamed the Fox. Vulpus, who the gossips said was nobly born.

Titus had arranged with the new Procurator, replacing Scipius who had died the previous day after a lingering and painful illness, finally succumbing to a bloody flux, that Marcus should fight against another rising gladiator, named Bulmerius. A young man whose innocent young face hid a ferocious and bestial nature.

"He will test you, Marcus, but I think that your speed will yet win through. There is naught to gain by matching you only with elderly fighters or boys fresh to the arena."

So it was to be. The morning was devoted to displays with animals and the midday break to the execution of several minor criminals, each man dispatching the previous one, helping to put the capacity audience into the right bloodthirsty frame of mind.

Then it was time for Ragnar to take to the sand, marching alongside the tall Atascadorus. They were a startling contrast and the mob applauded them as they entered. Titus stood up in the Imperial Box to take their salutes, smiling with pleasure at the response from the people. Marcus was waiting for his turn, wearing no armor, his sword strapped to his side. For he was to fight Bulmerius in the Samnite fashion. Both armed with shield and sword.

The plebians, packed in row upon row, mainly wearing cloaks of dull brown, stood and roared on their own choice. Most favored Atascadorus, for he had already won the wooden staff of freedom, and was known as a doughty and skilled fighter.

But this odd Northman!

Taller than any man they'd seen since the Parthian giant of four years back. And he had been a mighty failure. Matched against a pair of dwarfs who had simply cut through his legs out of his gangling reach, and hewn him down like a rotten tree.

But this Ragnar was something different from that. Still disdaining any armor, he carried the net flung casually over his arm like a cast-off robe in a heat wave, and he hefted the long trident easily under his left arm, as though he was about to go fishing with a willow switch.

His skin was still as pale as milk, and his brushed silver hair was tied loosely back with a colored ribbon sent him by a lady admirer.

By his side the polished skin of Atascadorus seemed blacker than ever. And the Nubian's teeth more white in that grinning face. He carried his helmet under his arm, his short stabbing sword still in its sheath.

"Morituri te salutant," they called out together. At

91

least Ragnar was respecting the conventions this time. Titus gravely acknowledged their salute, sitting down again, his eyes roaming among the marble seats of the rich, seeing that all three of his protégé's enemies were there. The cousins, Gellius and Vitruvius, sitting together with their wives. And a miserable-looking Vellius Condorus, huddled under a great fur coat, in the seats reserved for visiting dignitaries from the further parts of the Empire.

Helped by two other Nubians, the great Atascadorus donned his helmet. Presented to him by a group of his supporters, who had won four and a half thousand aurei on his last combat, the helm was decorated with birds and animals, each one engraved and ornamented in gold and silver, while the leaping dolphin on top of the helmet was made of solid silver, a plume of purple feathers spouting from it.

It covered his entire face, with only a narrow slit for the eyes. Atascadorus carried a plain shield, with only a simple design of crossed spears at its center. He selected his sword from five or six offered to him by his servants, swinging and balancing them, until he found one to his satisfaction. Finally, the armor for the right arm was buckled on, and he was ready.

During the preparations, Marcus had been watching closely, studying the black, in case he ever had to fight the man. "A grain of inside knowledge is worth a sack full of muscles," was one of Argos's favorite sayings.

Marcus also watched his friend Ragnar, who stood over to one side, ignoring his opponent, seeming to be talking to himself, shuffling his feet. Hunching his shoulders, his head moving on his thick neck. It was strange the affinity that the young Roman felt for the tall barbarian, ever since they had first met. Finding companionship in each other that they seemed to find impossible with any other.

And yet, at the back of Marcus's mind were the words of the Emperor. "To be a successful fighter for the crowds is like being the Emperor of Rome. You can afford no friends and no enemies. In the arena, there will come a time, be it sooner or later, when you will have to make a choice. Between a friend, and life."

But not yet, thought Marcus. Not today. If Ragnar could manage to defeat this Atascadorus, and he could beat young Bulmerius, then they would be both be well set on the path toward success. In front of the Emperor, in the last major Games of the year, with the seats filled to bursting.

And after that . . . ? After that, if they both won through, it should be possible to arrange matters so that they were not drawn against each other. No Procurator or lanista wanted to risk losing one or both of his top attractions.

Out in the arena, all of the preliminaries were at last over. Atascadorus withdrew a few paces, his head cocked on one side so that he could see the Imperial Box and the signal to fight. Ragnar also watched for the dropping of the hand, his trident held loosely at hip level.

There was a great roar from the crowd as the Imperial hand fell, in a sharp cutting gesture.

Atascadorus moved in quickly, trying the usual trick against inexperienced gladiators of catching them unprepared and off balance. Ragnar's response brought a sudden shocked silence from the mob, followed by a mixture of jeers and excited applause.

Instead of using the net as a retiarius was supposed to, swirling it to draw the mormillo in and then tangle his feet, Ragnar had simply slipped the knot off his wrist and thrown it at Atascadorus, making him duck and then stand back in total disbelief. It was against the accepted methods and etiquette of the arena, and the Nubian was bewildered by it.

Marcus shook his head in disbelief as he watched his friend further ignore all the rules of fighting with net and trident. Instead of holding the three-pronged spear far down the shaft and jabbing his opponent, the albino had changed his grip, his hands right at the long end of the shaft. Swinging it in a hissing arc of death, as though it was some oddly shaped axe.

"He fights foul!" bellowed a hoarse voice from the front rows of boxes. Coming, Marcus thought, from a muffled figure he recognized.

"No!" roared another voice. Backed up by more cries. The mob loved something out of the ordinary, and Ragnar was certainly that.

Marcus realized that his friend might, perhaps by accident, have stumbled upon his best chance of defeating the mighty Atascadorus. The gladiator had been fighting in the arena for years, and was used to the formalization of the combats. And that could prove his undoing. Render him helpless against this wildly unconventional approach from the towering Northman.

Indeed the black was giving ground, trying to fend off the lethal swings of the trident with his sword, but Ragnar's strength was so great that he was in danger of having it knocked from his hands. And when he ducked behind the shield, the ringing blows brought louder cheers from the crowds all around, most of whom were already up on their feet with the excitement.

Atascadorus turned his head wildly, trying to work out exactly where he was in the arena, realizing that he was being herded into one of the narrower angles, close to the Gate of Libitina. He tried to feint to the left, dodging right, to get away from the hissing circle of the trident. But the deep red eyes of the Northman followed him, picking up every move. Ragnar was beautifully balanced on the balls of his feet, shifting sideways to close off the avenue of escape, pushing the Nubian further and further back.

"Mithras! He can take him!" breathed Marcus, watching every moment of the battle.

Again the gladiator tried to cut away the trident, bracing his sword against the blow, but misjudging the angle, so that the shaft slid down the sword, glancing off to rip a gaping flesh wound under the ribs on the right side.

"Habet!" roared the crowd in delight, and the betting redoubled on the Northman.

Atascadorus staggered, nearly dropping the heavy shield, letting his head drop behind cover. A shade late, for the next cut of the trident neatly hacked away the rippling plume atop the silver dolphin. Bringing another cheer from the mob.

The black found the unbelievable happening. Feeling the sudden chill of the metal grille around the perimeter of the arena, rough against his bare back. There was nowhere else to run to.

Waving his sword in an unconvincing impression of aggression, Atascadorus ducked lower behind the shield. And Ragnar saw his chance. Checked his swing in mid-blow, ramming the triple point at the legs of his opponent. At the last second Atascadorus spotted it, and tried to leap over the attack, but was just a hair's breadth too late. The one hooked tip caught him in the muscular part of the calf, bringing more blood, and sending him hopping off balance.

Ragnar whipped the long-shafted trident upward, locking it behind the shield, then tugging hard. Wrenching it from the black's hands, pulling it clear away, leaving Atascadorus unprotected. The crowd

95

quietened momentarily, sensing the kill was near, then cheering as the older man made a marvelous recovery, cutting at the trident, snapping the wood clean in two.

Ragnar threw the broken end in his opponent's face, diving under for the end with the metal points, rolling over and back up on his feet, ready to fight, while Atascadorus was still trying to regain his balance, weighing up whether it was worth trying for his shield. Deciding it wasn't.

The pair were fairly evenly matched again, though the Nubian was bleeding copiously from his two wounds. The one under the ribs and the other in the leg. And he was sufficiently experienced to know that time was no longer on his side.

Ragnar closed on Atascadorus, still holding the broken trident as if it were a fighting axe of his people, swinging it at the black's face, making him step back again, his short sword outranged.

It happened so fast, that Marcus could only guess what his friend had done. One moment the Nubian was defending himself stoutly with the gladius, and the next moment it had vanished from his hand. Ragnar had fenced at him with the trident, until he was able to twist it sharply, trapping the short sword between two of the prongs, dragging it out of the hand of Atascadorus, sending it spinning high in the air, to fall in the sand thirty or forty paces away.

There was no more wagers. Nobody likes to bet on a dead man, and everyone there knew that the big black was doomed. He had entered the arena as the hero. Their favorite. A man who could have taken his freedom and bought land anywhere in the Empire and lived out the remainder of his days in quiet and happiness.

Instead he was running. Running for his life. Head

thrown back, sweat streaming down the inside of the ornamental helmet, fleeing in blind panic for his life. The jeers and laughter of the crowd swilling about him. And Ragnar running lightly after him, the ribbon fallen from his hair, so that it spread out behind him like a shimmering banner.

Marcus joined in the shouting, watching as Ragnar chased his opponent. Once. Twice. Three times around the outside of the arena, never bothering to try and cut across in front of him to shorten the contest.

Marcus realized how good Atascadorus must have been when he saw him manage three complete circuits of the Ampitheater without stumbling. Knowing the gut-ripping fear that must be clutching at him. Seeing Ragnar close effortlessly with him, his teeth pulled back in a grimace of animal pleasure.

As they passed near him for the third time, Marcus saw with a slight disquiet that there was white froth on Ragnar's lips, and that his eyes seemed to be staring blankly ahead of him, as though he were in some kind of trance.

Just in front of the Imperial Box on the fourth time around, the black tried to turn his head to look up at Titus, half-raising his hand in appeal. But wearing that heavy helmet, it was a dangerous move.

A fatal move.

His feet betrayed him, and he fell headlong, banging his chin a fearful blow in the hard-packed sand, rolling over on his back. Ragnar was close at his heels, still holding the trident in his right hand.

The fallen Nubian made a brief effort to rise on his elbow, to make his appeal to the yelling crowd and to the watching Emperor. The mob would have howled him down after that panicky run for his life, but it is just possible that Titus might have spared him.

Ragnar wasn't about to allow anyone else the choice of whether an enemy lived or not. He planted one foot in the center of the black's chest, pressing him flat on his back. Placed the triple-pointed trident carefully through the narrow slit in the front of that rich helmet, with as much concentration as a woman threading a needle, and when it was positioned to his satisfaction, ignoring a low bubbling moan from Atascadorus, he leaned his weight against the broken end of the shaft.

The body thrashed as the points vanished from sight, and blood swelled up, flowing out of the eyeholes, running down through the gap under the chin, spreading out in a great muddy pool around the dying man. Ragnar set both hands to the shaft, grinding it home, grimacing with the effort. Marcus guessed that the two outside tines had each penetrated through an eyeball while the center one was grating on the hard bone of the black's forehead.

At last the body was still, and Ragnar stood up, his foot on its chest, and gave out a great ringing war cry, ferocious enough to chill the blood. Leaving the splintered end of wood stuck through the skull of the Nubian, Ragnar walked toward the Imperial Box, picking up the dead man's sword as he did so, his eyes fixed on Titus.

The crowd were going wild as they acknowledged a new champion, throwing down coins into the sand, all of which the Northman ignored. Two attendants came scampering toward him, intending to drag out the body and begin to tidy up ready now for Marcus's fight. But as they neared him, Ragnar turned on them, shouting out a great cry in his own tongue. One of the men turned tail instantly and ran.

The other, less wise, stood his ground and tried to speak to Ragnar. He might as well have tried to turn

Tiber in its course. With one great blow of the gladius, the tall albino split his head open, cleaving him from pate to nose, the brains spilling out in a gray torrent either side of the shining blade.

At this, the cheering faded away, and the mob grew puzzled. This wasn't right. It wasn't normal for the victor to slay a helpless slave like that. Ragnar ignored the cries as he had ignored the cheers, until he stood beneath the seats of the Imperial party.

When he began to shout, lifting his voice so that everyone there could hear him, including his friend, Marcus Julius Britannicus, who shuddered as though someone had just ridden over his grave.

"Is that your best man, Romans?" The arena had fallen to a stillness like a chamber of death as the crowd looked and listened at the strange figure, brandishing a bloody sword, with a bloody corpse at his feet.

"The best you can send? Back home our maidens would spit upon such a warrior and mock him, and he would be set to cleaning out the midden!"

There was the beginning of an angry mutter.

"When I was taken, by treachery, I and my five brothers, we slew a hundred of your mighty soldiers. Thirty did I slay myself. And they were puking children. As are all of you Romans. Cowards and children!"

"No!" The cry came from a thousand throats at this gross insult to Rome and her proud people.

Marcus shook his head sadly as he saw the strange fighting madness had possessed his friend. His speech was becoming thicker and more barbarous, and he threw his head from side to side, the wind picking at his white hair.

"I challenge you! All of you. Your stinking cock

there of an Emperor! Come down and kiss my sword and we will talk of what truly makes a man!"

In his Box, Marcus saw Titus half-rise to his feet as though he would take the words of this barbarian and ram them back down his throat. And from what he knew of his Emperor, Marcus had no doubt that Titus had at least the courage to attempt it. But a gray-haired man at his side drew him down, whispering something in his ear.

"So you are afeared. By Odin, but there are no men there. I will fight you all. Any man who wishes death then let him step down to me, and the wound dew shall flow and the maidens shall fly loaded to the sky hall. Come! Come!"

Ragnar's voice rose to a maddened scream, and as Marcus looked on, unable to move to either help or hinder, he saw his friend rip off his breech-clout, and stand quite naked in front of the great crowd.

In a seat near the front a gracious lady, the wife of the merchant Helvius Geminus, found herself nearly fainting with a delicious mixture of fear and lust for the great white body of the Northman.

Most of the mob were on their feet, but this time it was anger and not excitement that roused them. If it had not been for the high wall and the barrier of iron that was built to protect them from the wild animals, they would have poured down into the arena and overwhelmed the lone Northman like an avalanche of rage.

But still Ragnar stood, braving the Emperor in a way that had never been known. A dozen members of the Imperial bodyguard had appeared at the side of Titus, all holding the throwing javelin, but no order came for them to use them. Nor to the archers that had worked their way to the front of the seats, arrows notched.

"I say that each Roman is a coward. Each Roman is a whore-born coward and your gods are not worth the filth in the gutter."

Over to one side the crowd had stopped their angry calls and had begun to cheer, and Marcus was quickly able to see why. And seeing why, he turned and began to make his way as fast as he could toward the Box where Titus sat, brushing aside any man who attempted to check him.

Ragnar also turned at the disturbance, his face changing to a weird smile, many times more frightening that his grimace of hatred. "So there is still a Roman who will not crawl on his belly like a dog!"

Having jumped down the great wall, he saw a young man scrambling up and over the iron fence. A wealthy Tribune, having come to enjoy a day at the Games, having downed three amphorae of wine, had grabbed his sword and was ready and willing to defend his honor and the honor of his Emperor.

Encouraged by his example, three others followed him, all rich. All young. Mostly a little drunk.

Four men, advancing toward the lone, naked figure of the white-skinned man, standing waiting at the center of the great arena.

To the inexperienced eyes of many there, it was clearly going to be an unfair contest.

To the experienced eyes of a few of the men there, it was clearly going to be an unfair contest.

Marcus had nearly reached the Imperial Box, out of breath from his hurried dash, when the fight began.

The Northman was in a battle frenzy, whirling like a maddened top, screaming out threats and oaths in a high-pitched voice, swirling the blade in a whistling circle, wide red eyes glaring at the approaching young men, who looked nervously at each other, suddenly feeling their mouths dry and the palms of their hands damp with sweat.

And their seats seemed very far away.

And very safe.

The yelling from the crowd had stopped and the Amphitheater was quieter than Marcus had ever heard it, each spectator perched on the edge of his seat.

It was all very quick.

Had the young men concerted their attack, all coming in at Ragnar at once, then they might have stood some sort of chance. Perhaps only one, or at worst two, of them might have died.

Not all four.

The first came in hesitantly, looking for one of the others to support him. Ragnar saw the hesitation, and struck first, his blade blurring in and out so fast that the eye blinked, suspecting some sort of trick. But the young Tribune lay on the sand, his legs kicking, hands clutching a ferocious gash in his abdomen, eyes squeezed shut with pain.

The second saw him fall and rushed in, sword raised, a heroic battle cry on his lips. Ragnar parried the gladius with contemptuous ease, chopping the Roman across the neck with the oak-hard edge of his mighty left hand, tripping the falling man. Spinning and plunging his own keen point between the shoulder blades, severing the spinal column, bringing an instant and total darkness.

When the third and fourth saw the brutal ease with which the Northman dispatched their comrades, they looked at each other, and began to circle, intending to bewilder him with their cunning.

While they moved, one attempted to unfasten his cloak, perhaps hoping to use it as a retiarius would his net. But the brooch at his neck proved stubborn, and he paused to free it.

His eyes were still fixed to the awkward fastening, fingers scrabbling at it, when he felt a fierce pain in his stomach, and he saw the flash of a sword as it was withdrawn from his body. As he fell forward, Ragnar hit him again, the second blow thrusting through the young man's heart, killing him instantly. Even while his body lay bleeding on the sand, the Roman's hands still groped to unfasten his cloak, the muscles trying to obey the last message of the dying brain.

Marcus was at the side of the Emperor, pausing to watch the scene of carnage in the arena, just as the fourth and last of the attackers fell to the naked Northman. Halfway committed to his assault, he had checked as he saw his only surviving comrade so swiftly and easily butchered, and that moment's hesitation was all that Ragnar needed. To counter the feeble cut of the gladius, and to kick out, knocking the young man staggering sideways. Following him and remorselessly hewing him down, still hacking at the corpse even after the head was quite severed from the trunk.

After a moment of total stillness, the crowd went wild, the women screaming and shouting, while the men stood and hurled abuse. But Marcus noticed that nobody seemed inclined to follow the brave example of the four young men who now lay still in the packed sand, their blood congealing into dull pools. While Ragnar stalked the arena, flourishing his sword over his head and shouting insults at the baying mob.

Titus turned his head and saw Marcus standing there at his elbow and beckoned him over, placing his lips near to the young Roman's ear.

"You come to ask for mercy for your friend?"

"I come to ask that I may be allowed to try and

talk with him, my Emperor. The madness had possessed him and he knows not what he does or where he is."

Titus shook his head. Marcus could see that he was in a bitter rage, his hands trembling with the effort of maintaining his self-control before all the attendants.

"I will do better, for you. Marcus Julius Britannicus, I will do better. You may spare him from the punishment that the slave dog so richly deserves. In a moment I shall order archers into the arena, and they will shoot his legs full of arrows from a safe distance. When he is down and helpless, I shall have him bound."

"What then, my Emperor? Has he not shown great courage this day?"

Titus laughed, but his eyes remained cold and bitter. "Aye. A fine courage that leaves a great gladiator dead. A harmless attendant with his brains puddled in the dirt, and four of the flower of young Rome slain. And the crowd angrier than I have ever known them."

"But, my Emperor . . ."

Fingers gripped his arm with such power that he winced, but Titus tightened them still more. "Marcus, you are my man. And you will do what I command you. There is not time for a lengthy discussion of who is right or wrong. I will have the man butchered in the most agonizing public manner I can conceive, so that he will be days a dying. And all the world will know what happens to a cur who braves the might of Rome. Or . . ."

Marcus felt a sickness come to him, and his head swam as he saw ahead what Titus would say to him. It was as certain as the sun braving the east tomorrow's morn.

"Or you will kill him. As quickly and as skillfully as you know how. He is a dead man, my Vulpus. All you must do is decide the manner of his passing."

There was no decision to be made.

Although Marcus was not yet dressed in armor, he carried his sword, and that was all he needed. Against a man who wore nothing, it might well be a disadvantage to be slowed down at all. Making sure his gladius was firmly in its sheath, he stepped to the front of the Imperial Box, resting his hand on the marble balustrade.

"The Gods go with you, Marcus," said Titus, leaning forward on his seat.

The young Roman vaulted nimbly over, dropping on his feet behind the iron fence, ignoring the calls from the crowd. Climbing up the barrier, and shinning quickly down the other side, not wanting to risk being caught by the berserk Northman, halfway up.

"It's Vulpus!" he heard a voice call out. "Vulpus! He'll stick the swine!!"

"Vulpus!"

"It's Vulpus, the Fox!"

"Go at him, Vulpus!!"

He was surprised that so many took up the cry, and tried to blank them out from his mind, concentrating only on what he had to do. The jeers faded away as the spectators saw a new champion stride out to do battle for the name and honor of Rome.

Ragnar, his back turned to the Imperial Box, still ranted at the mob, hacking at one of the corpses to emphasize his hatred of all things Roman. Marcus walked within a dozen paces of him, the cheers swelling in the rows of seats, before he called out to the Northman.

"Hó, Ragnar, my brother!"

Slowly, blinking like a bear caught in its winter sleep, the great figure turned his head, the red eyes gleaming with blind hatred. Marcus realized with a shudder that Ragnar didn't recognize him, the fighting madness darkening a part of his mind.

"Another dog, come to be taught a lesson about the cowards that people this stinking city!"

"Ragnar! It is I. Marcus Julius Britannicus. Your friend and brother."

The noise was fading again, as the crowd watched in bewilderment, wondering why the battle didn't begin, unable to hear the exchange.

The massive white head shook, the silver hair shimmering about it. "Marcus. That name comes from the cavern of my past. A memory not worth the remembering."

"We must fight, Ragnar, my brother, or the Romans will cripple you and make you a mewling thing to be mocked by their women and children. It must be."

"All time is one, my brother." The eyes no longer glittered with the fierce light of madness, and the voice was quieter. "And so you and I, brothers under this cold sun, must fight, and the ravens will pick the white bones of the loser as he sleeps with the old gray widowmaker. It has come to this, then?"

"I owe you a life. All I can do, my brother, is to fight and so spare you a far worse ending."

"Then come!" shouted the Northman, leaping forward, the short stabbing sword swinging in a great cut at Marcus's head.

The Roman was just in time to bring up his own blade and counter, feeling the shock of the impact jar his arm clear to the shoulder. Retreating a few paces, fending off the attacks as best he could. Part of his mind horrified by the speed and strength of the big man. The other part wondering how to beat him.

He glimpsed Titus, his face pale and strained, staring fixedly down from the Imperial Box. Heard the cries of encouragement from the stands. Felt the sand beneath his sandals, watching for the bodies that lay haggled around the arena, taking care not to trip over them.

Twice Ragnar had lunged at him and missed, out of range by a hand's span, and Marcus recalled the workouts in the Ludus. And his advice to his friend to remember that the Roman sword was one of the shortest weapons in the world. The swords that the Northman was used to would be far longer. Which was why, despite his greater reach, Ragnar was missing him.

It hung on his lips to warn his friend about this fault, then realized that it would be fruitless. This combat was to the death, and there could be no avoiding it. And in such a situation, Marcus could do only one thing.

Ducked under the next wild swing, his own point licking out at the naked body, drawing a plume of blood from the ribs on the left side of the chest. Making Ragnar hesitate. Marcus himself unable to strike again, watching the blood flow with fascination. It was the first time that he had seen the tall albino wounded. and he had looked for the blood to be white, and yet it was as red as any man's.

"Habet!" Louder than he had ever heard it.

The Northman rallying, coming in again, but the edge of speed had gone, and the blow was parried. It held less force than before and Marcus countered and struck back, wounding his friend again, this time high on the left arm, cutting the muscle. Though Ragnar

107

quickly changed hands, Marcus hit him again, plunging his own sword deep in under the feeble attempt at defense. Slitting open the muscular stomach. Out, and again in, this time higher.

Stepping back amid a wall of sound from the spectators, watching the end. Not hearing the cries of acclamation for "Vulpus! Vulpus, the Fox!"

Only knowing that he had been forced to kill one of the few people that he had ever truly liked, and feeling sick to his heart.

Dropping his own bloodstained sword to the sand, and kneeling beside Ragnar, wondering at how small and frail he had suddenly become, as he knelt there in the arena, both hands pressed to his chest.

"You have slain me, Marcus, my brother," said the Northman, his voice soft.

"Aye, brother. That fault of under reaching. I told you it would be the end of you."

A thin smile came to the bloodless lips, and Ragnar coughed. "Truly. And I thought not to hear the old woman calling me for many a year."

Marcus reached out and held the dying man in his arms, feeling tears prick at his eyes.

"No more shall I hold a maiden and lie with her on a summer beach while the seals cry. It is sad to die so young. Farewell, Marcus."

"Farewell, Ragnar."

"Farewell, brother."

He felt the spirit depart from the flesh, leaving only an empty husk, and he rose to his feet, picking up his sword, saluting the smiling Titus, letting the shouts carry him from the arena.

"Vulpus! Vulpus! Hail Vulpus. Hail Vulpus!"

And he thought yet again of the words of Titus. "In the arena, there will come a time, be it sooner or later, when you will have to make a choice. Between a friend, and life."

Marcus had made the choice, and would live with it forever.

EIGHT

Overnight, Marcus Julius Britannicus, Vulpus the Fox, had become the darling of Rome. Everyone had heard of him, and he was inundated with invitations to attend dinners in his honor, and every politician came with offers for him to fight.

And there were the women, sending their servants with messages. Some ambiguous. Some not.

But all that moved him was revenge.

He had the love and protection of Titus, and he had been richly rewarded for killing Ragnar. The Emperor still kept Vellius Condorus at arm's length, urging him to shepherd his health and to call at the Palace only when he was fully recovered. But by all accounts his illness grew worse.

It was only two days after Marcus's triumph when he received, among many others, an invitation to the house of Metellus Julius Vitruvius. He learned that there would be a sumptuous meal, and the guests would be allowed to see a wonderful new flour mill put into operation that would be the envy of all rich men. Powered by a mule, one massive block of stone, that had taken a month to ferry to the house, ground slowly around in an enclosed pit, and the crushed flour cascaded down a chute into vats.

Vitruvius was very proud of it.

"It will be a trap."

"I know, my Emperor. But it is said that often it is the hunter who becomes the hunted. I shall go there, and if there is to be an attack on me, then . . . well, it will not be the first time. And I still live."

Titus shivered, tugging his cloak closer around his broad shoulders. Marcus noticed that the Emperor's hair was becoming streaked with gray.

"I freeze here in Rome. My feet are like blocks hewn from Tiber's ice."

"They say, my Emperor, that a cure for that is to soak one's feet in boiled turnips."

"Boiled turnips! I think, my boy, that I would rather have the cold feet!"

Despite his optimism with Titus, Marcus went to the great house on the northern outskirts of the Eternal City, with some trepidation. There wasn't much doubt in his mind that it was a trick. That both Vitruvius and Gellius would be there. And that they would try and have him killed. He thought that if there was to be an assassination attempt then it would most likely come from the two cousins, rather than through hired swords. The name of Vulpus was too well known at that moment for them to hope to keep men's lips sealed with bribes.

But he was prepared. He wore his gladius under his cloak, and carried two small daggers, hidden in soft

111

leather sheaths. One at the nape of his neck, hidden by the high collar of his woolen tunic. The other strapped to his left forearm, under the tunic's long sleeves.

The slaves at the door held bright torches, and there was a great bowl of steaming hot water in the middle of the atrium, for him to both wash and warm his hands. The mansion was bustling with noise and merriment, and men flocked around him to touch him and hope to bring themselves luck.

His host for the evening, Metellus Julius Vitruvius, came toward him, walking with an unsteady and false bonhomie, a rosy smile pasted across his triple chins, gripping Marcus by the forearm and enveloping him in the heady fumes of Cyprian wine.

"My dearest boy, may I call you "Vulpus?" How sweet of you to come to our little evening. We shall be dining in a while, and then I propose to have a grand opening of my new mill in the garden. It will be quite, quite thrilling."

A sour-faced matron stood at his elbow, sniffing at Marcus, waiting for her husband to introduce her.

"Ah, my little Flavia. This is the gallant hero of the Games who slew the giant Northman. Marcus Julius Britannicus, though men now call him Vulpus."

"The Fox. An unusual name for a butcher. And you kill for the Emperor, I believe."

Marcus realized that the woman, uniquely for a high-born Roman lady in public, was drunk. Despite his own befuddled state, Vitruvius also realized it and grabbed her by the arm, tugging her away. Though it was done with an apparent husbandly concern, Marcus saw the livid weals that sprang up on Flavia's arm where he had held her. And she vanished in the direction of her own rooms and did not reappear until after the meal.

Vitruvius came back immediately to Marcus shooing away a group of nobles who had surrounded him again. "A thousand apologies. My wife is not well. She did not mean what she said to you. She is among your greatest admirers. But such a strong-willed woman. Like her mother, I am sorry to say. But let it pass. Let it pass."

Marcus let it pass.

The meal was superb. The finest food that Marcus had ever tasted. But the company was not to his liking. Setting aside that his host was a man he intended to kill as soon as possible, the rest were rich hangers-on. Fawners and toadies, who laughed at every jest of Vitruvius. Laughing even as the scurra went around the table, telling scandalous stories about everyone present.

Except Marcus.

There were two notable absentees from the feast. The cousin, Gellius. And Vellius Condorus.

Marcus had not dared to ask Vitruvius about either of them, in case his suspicions were, in fact, not yet aroused. But another hoggish guest supplied him with the answers.

"Condorus is still unwell. They say his trip across Gaul has brought him out in a winter fever. Unless it's something he's caught from those pagans out in Britannia. And Gellius is . . . Charon take me if I know where he is. I'm sure he was about earlier."

A slave brought Marcus the message he had been half-expecting. Many of the guests were sunk into drunken sleep, or busy evacuating their stomachs at the vomitarium, ready for a further assault on the spreading dishes of viands. He noticed that Vitruvius watched him as the message arrived, and the warning signal sent a prickle down his spine.

113

Scratched hastily on a tablet with what looked like a splintered and blunt stylus, or even perhaps a jagged fingernail, it was short and to the point.

"The Legate of the Valeria Victrix Legion is gone. I know how."

It was not signed.

The Legate of the Legion that the message named was, of course, Lucian Julius Britannicus. The father of Marcus.

Muttering an excuse to his neighbor, Marcus stretched himself from the couch and made his way out of the smoke-filled room, bowing at the door to his host.

Who called out to him, "Leaving us, Vulpus?"

"No, Julius Vitruvius. I am feeling fatigued and would walk a while in the cool night air."

"Then take care not to catch a chill, Vulpus. We would not wish to lose you."

Marcus followed the slave out through the doors, closing them behind him. "Where? And who gave you the message? Tell me."

The slave shook his head. "My master tell me to tell you to meet him by forge beyond fish pool. He tell me to say no more or he will kill me."

If Marcus had not been so sure of the sender of the message, he would have forced the slave to talk.

But he was. And so did not.

The garden was dark, the stars glittering high over his head, in a clear, frost-bearing sky. Among the trees Vitruvius had dotted numerous fish pools, and Marcus saw that ice gave a dull sheen to the water. He also saw a small light gleaming over the far side of the land, well away from the house.

Far enough away for nobody in the house to hear any noise. Any screams.

As he walked closer, his hand resting easily on the hilt of his sword, Marcus saw the light came from the partly open shutter on a square building. Solidly built of brick, with a heavy door.

From the chimney on top he guessed that this must be the forge where he was to meet . . . who?

Or what?

He felt frost crackling beneath his sandals as he drew closer. Wondering how and when the attack would come. By now he was totally convinced that he was walking into a trap. It would have been easy to have gone back, to safety. Left the house of Vitruvius. And waited for another chance on another day. But that was not his way. Now he was there, with two of the men who had destroyed his father, then it would be foolish to leave.

The door stood ajar and he pushed it cautiously, so that it swung open, revealing the interior of the building. A great anvil, and various hammers had bellows revealed that it was the forge. A small fire smoldered amid a heap of glowing ashes at the center of the room.

Apart from that, there was nobody there.

Marcus paused in the doorway, silhouetted against the yellow light of a torch on the wall of the forge. Waiting.

"Move a step and I feather this shaft in your back."

The voice was quiet, only a little above a whisper. With a tremble to it that might be fear. Or age. The young Roman knew that he made a perfect target, but he had banked on the would-be killer wanting to talk a little before he struck. Marcus was not a fool, and he had lived long enough to know that men of power, like the Emperor Titus, did few good deeds for nothing. If the Emperor had given him the names of these four men, then there was a fair chance that he personally had some reason for wanting them dead. Perhaps his agents had brought whispers of ice. And there cannot be ice without water. So, if there was a plot, then the conspirators would want to learn what was known.

"Keep your hands from your sword, Vulpus. None of your fox's tricks here. And stand very still. I could bring down a goose on the wing when I was a boy, and my hand has lost little of its skill."

"Come forward, Lucius Julius Gellius, so that I may see you clearly. I would not want to die without seeing the man who ruined my father."

"You will see it, and it will be the last thing that you look upon, you murderous dog."

"I murderous? The coward slays with a whisper. It is the brave man who kills with a sword."

"Walk inside, and try none of your arena tricks. Or you will die a while earlier."

The one thing that Marcus needed to know before he made a move was whether the noble was alone. If he were not, and there was more than one bow drawn at his back, then to attempt to fight would bring immediate death. Stood against the light as he was, even the worst of archers could hardly fail to hit him.

Carefully, not making any sudden moves, Marcus stepped inside the forge, walking across to stand by the smoldering fire, taking care not to step on the great pair of bellows on the floor.

He heard the door being closed and the noise of feet moving to the window, and the tugging home of the shutters.

"There. Now we are free from any interruption. You may turn around. Slowly!"

Marcus was shocked. The men who had killed his mother had been mainly young. Barely older than he was. Isidorus was not a young man, and Vitruvius was

116

well into middle-age. But Gellius was old. Old, and bald and flabby. His cheeks lined and his fringe of hair white. And the fingers that gripped the hunting bow were gnarled and crooked.

The point of the arrow was aimed at the center of Marcus's chest, but it trembled like an aspen tree in a summer breeze. The greatest danger seemed to be that he would loose the shaft by accident.

"Marcus Julius Britannicus."

"Lucius Julius Gellius."

"I think that you have been looking for me."

Marcus shook his head. "I did not know it until a few days past. Yet I have searched for you and the others for near ten years. Since my father killed himself. Why did you do it? I am truly curious. He was a good man. Not filled with pride or ambition. Why?"

The old man shook his head. "It is so long past and gone. We were younger, and there were matters that we wished to put forward. That would have aided us. By his damned morality, your father stopped us. I doubt he realized what he had done. But we were near ruined by his honesty. We had paid his price, so we made sure that the traitor dog paid ours."

"He was no traitor!"

"Yes. Else he would not have killed himself as he did. He should not have married a woman who was not of Rome. It was that we used to bring him low."

Marcus shook his head. This venomous old man with his ancient hatreds was fit only to be put down, as you would slit the throat of an old hunting dog when it could no longer run with the pack and follow a scent.

Yet the memory of his father's wretched and lonely end fueled the fires of his anger, and he determined to make Gellius suffer a little before ending his life.

"Before I kill you, Marcus, there are a few questions that we would like answered. Answer them well, and it may even be that we shall let you live. If you give us your word to leave Rome forever."

It would have been interesting to know what these questions were, but Marcus guessed that Vitruvius might appear at any moment, and it would be hard to fight clear with two of them there.

"Well enough."

"What? You must speak louder, my boy, for my ears are not as sharp as they once were."

Gellius stepped closer, still holding the bow fully drawn, though the effort was considerable and his arms shook. By moving closer, as Marcus had hoped he would, he placed himself right against the smoldering fire of the forge. Marcus risked a glance down, seeing that his foot was only a hand's span from the leather bellows.

"I said that you looked cold and that I would try and *warm you!*"

He stamped hard on the bellows, throwing himself sideways immediately, hoping that the smith had left them connected to the fire.

He had.

There was a great gush of air through the pipe, bursting up under the embers, making them erupt in a cloud of fire and red-hot ash, which enveloped Gellius at its center. He shouted out, the shock making him release the arrow that hissed through the air and buried itself in a wooden shelf at the back of the forge.

"No!" he screamed, beating out flames that licked at the hem of his cloak, filling the small room with the stench of burning wool.

Marcus powered himself up from the crouch, hitting the older man around the knees, sending him crashing on his back in the dirt. The breath whooshed

118

from Gellius's lungs and he lay still, fighting for air, mouth working desperately.

Seeing that he was no threat, Marcus stood up, brushing dust from his cloak. Checking automatically that his sword was still in its scabbard. Revenge was at hand, and he was not going to waste time on it.

"Get up you pathetic bag of tripes, before I spit you on the floor like the animal you are."

"Please. Mercy for an old man."

"I show you the mercy that you showed my father. You and the others. Isidorus is dead. Now you. Then your cousin, and finally Condorus. I have a double score to settle with that one."

"Gold. Women. Boys. Anything."

"Gellius; I have but one desire, and that is to see you die slowly and alone. Before Vitruvius comes I intend to see to it. Now stand."

Lucius Julius Gellius collapsed weeping, crying on his ancestors to spare him, but no aid came. Marcus dragged him roughly to his feet, leaning him against the end wall of the small building, while he looked around for suitable instruments for vengeance. And his mind went back to the slaughter of the followers of Spartacus, and he smiled.

Gellius saw him smile, and sobbed, his fat shoulders shaking.

There was an old box in one corner, and Marcus pulled it over and ordered Gellius to stand on it. The old man made a desperate dash for freedom, his pudgy fists flailing at Marcus. Who merely held his hands and laughed. Slapping the noble hard across the face, so the mark of his fingers stood out crimson against the pale flesh.

"Up there."

"Please. Will nothing turn you from your purpose? Is there nothing I can do?"

"Yes. As I have said, Gellius. You can die. Stand quite still. And open your mouth so that I can gag you."

The walls were thick enough and the forge far enough from the house for Marcus to be fairly safe. But there was no point when in the gardens of an enemy in taking any kind of unnecessary risk. He picked up a wad of torn cloth from the dirty floor and rammed it hard into Gellius's mouth, trying it tightly in place with a short length of rope.

"Put out your hand with the palm flat against the wall. Do it!"

But Gellius had seen him pick up the short, heavy hammer, and the handful of claw-headed nails. Each as long as a man's first finger.

In the end Marcus had to knot a loop of rope around the old man's neck, tying it to one of the low rafters of the gorge, to hold him upright while he worked with the hammer and the nails.

The ones through the center of the palms slid in easily, and Gellius suffered it with surprising calm, only trying to scream through the gag when Marcus used the hammer to bend the heads of the nails over, digging them into the soft flesh of the palm. As an additional safeguard, he drove two more nails through the center of each wrist, where they splintered bone and crushed tendons.

There was very little blood.

Twice the noble fainted, and twice Marcus slapped him back into consciousness, removing the rope from his neck. He had no wish for the man to be able to strangle himself and end the suffering quickly. Precariously balanced on the small box, with his arms crucified out straight, Gellius stared down at his tormentor with pain-filled eyes, sweat bubbling over his forehead and soaking into the gag. Blood dribbled down his chin where he had bitten either his lips or his tongue in his pain.

"Interesting, Lucius Julius Gellius. I'll wager that you've laughed many a time at the suffering of some poor bastard of a slave, crucified on a public highway as an example. I'm only sorry that I couldn't do this to you on the Via Appia so the people could mock you and pelt you with offal and dung."

The head moved slowly on the fat neck, the muscles corded with pain, as he tried to keep his balance. If he once fell then all his weight would flop on the nails through his hands and wrists.

"When Vitruvius comes to see how your questioning goes, he will, I think, be surprised at what he finds. He will find no answers. Just one more question. I am told that the end will come within hours. Sadly, nobody is likely to come here before the morning, so that will prove too late. Would you like to know what will happen?"

The eyes looked blankly at him, and Gellius made some sort of desperate kind of muffled groan. Perhaps he was trying to talk.

"Save your energy. And think on the suffering of my father. And what it meant to my mother. And to me. When a criminal is crucified, he has a ledge to rest his feet and take the weight from his hands. And there are normally ropes around the wrists. I believe that thirst is often a torment. To show mercy, the men who guard them can sometimes be persuaded to break their legs and speed their passing. Then their weight all falls on their arms. Like . . . so!"

And he kicked the box away, leaving Gellius suspended only by the nails. For a moment Marcus thought that the man's weight would pull him from the wall, but the forge was sturdily built, and the nails held.

There was a muffled scream through the gag, and the body writhed and kicked at the empty air. Then the eyes closed and Gellius went quite limp. Marcus wondered if the pain and shock had killed him, or whether he had simply fainted. In a moment he had the answer. The pain was such that it made the noble pass out, then the level of agony increased and brought him around again.

"I'm told that the pain will get no worse," he said, in a friendly conversational voice. "But it will begin again in a new way. By hanging forward like that, there is a great strain inside you. You can't quite draw in enough breath. Not quite. And so you struggle for the next breath. And the next. I'm told by men who know of these things that it'll be the breathing that kills you. Not anything else."

Each time Gellius recovered consciousness his head threw back in a rictus of agony, and his legs flailed at the box, just beyond his reach. Then he would faint, and the head would sag on the breast. Each time, he was visibly becoming weaker, and Marcus saw the old man would not live long. And he was strangely pleased. The death was enough for Gellius.

"Farewell, old man. I leave you to your thoughts. My father's shade will be pleased to see you."

And he left the forge, carefully blowing out the torch, and closing the door, leaving Gellius to die slowly, in darkness and alone.

NINE

Marcus had learned where this wonderful new mill was, and he thought it possible that Vitruvius might be checking out that all was well there before coming to see how his cousin was proceeding with the questioning of the gladiator, Vulpus.

As he walked quietly through the rambling grounds of the great house, Marcus looked up, seeing that cloud had drifted across the stars, although a sliver of moon was still visible, like a torch through a veil of gauze, hanging low in the sky. It was colder. The chill biting hard after the warmth of the forge, and he rubbed his hands together, keeping the blood flowing, knowing that at any moment he might be attacked and would need every nerve and muscle on the alert.

He walked around the end of a close-cropped hedge . . . straight into Metellus Julius Vitruvius, scurrying along a path, head down, chins tucked into his cloak against the frost. They actually bumped into each other hard, rebounding. The older man having just come from indoors and a bright light hadn't got his eyes adjusted to the darkness and rubbed himself.

"Clumsy oaf! Who in Hades is that, anyway? That's not you, Gellius, is it?"

Marcus didn't answer, knowing that if he made a sound his enemy would know who he was.

"I've just been running over things at the mill. All's ready. Just the trough to be filled with the meal, and then the lid clamped down. Do you know that my frigid-loined bitch of a wife has said she intends to stand beneath the spout and let the first flowing of flour run over her. Pah! She cares more about the money the mill will make for us than for me. Still, it will help with our design. Where is that traitor's son? Not dead already?"

"No. Not dead."

"Venus!"

"No. Not Venus. Vitruvius. That's the trow of a winner. And you're not a winner."

"Where is my cousin?"

Marcus laughed, the noise disturbing some night-burrowing creature that went scurrying through the long grass at the edge of the path.

"I had heard that your cousin was a secret follower of the Nazarene fish worshipper. Jesus Bar-Joseph."

"It cannot be true."

Marcus drew his sword, enough so that the other man could see the gleam of light on the blade and the whisper of metal as it left the scabbard.

"You call me a liar?"

"No. Of course. I am sure that you're right. Gellius was always a sly dog."

"I thought you would agree with me. So I treated him as we treated his Leader."

"But they crucified the Nazarene!"

124

"As I said . . . perhaps you are becoming hard of hearing . . . I treated him as we treated his Leader. I crucified him to the wall of the forge. He will still be there. Though I do not think he will be very alive by now."

Vitrivius turned his head, stooping away, and vomited. Heaving and gagging, crying as he did so. Ignoring the fact that the rank vomit splashed over his gown and sandals. Coughing and spluttering. Marcus waited calmly until he had finished retching. Watching him straighten and wipe the tears from his eyes with the edge of his cloak.

"There. Do you feel better now? Does the thought of death so upset you?"

"My cousin was an old man. With a wife and children. As do I."

Marcus stepped in close, longing to smash his fist into that well-fed smug face. "As did my father! You bastard!"

There had been two armed men on guard at the imposing tower of the new mill, but Metellus Julius Vitruvius had dismissed them, saying that he wanted a last hour before the mob of guests came flooding out of the house, rooted from every warm corner by slaves. To attend the grand opening, when the first batch of flour would be ground.

"And tell them no man is to enter here again. That I shall have everything ready as I arranged. Now go, before I have you both flogged!"

There was an almost hysterical note of anger in their master's voice, and the sentries were glad to scamper away to the warmth. Where they duly passed on the message to the senior house slave. It was well known that Vitruvius had placed great store by his new mill, and so his odd behavior seemed reasonable.

Back by the mill, Marcus followed closely behind the noble as they walked inside. Only when the door was slammed firmly shut and he knew they were alone did he remove the point of the dagger from the small of Vitruvius's back and return it to its sheath.

"That was well done. And they know that you would wish to operate the mill yourself?"

"Aye. I have given a year of my life to this venture. Not a light bargain when you reach my age. If you ever do reach my age."

"Listen, old man, and listen well to my words. So that you may not die in ignorance. My father died because of the web of lies spun by four men. Two are dead. You are the third. And tomorrow I shall visit the house of Vellius Condorus."

"He is sick."

"I shall make him a deal sicker."

"I am not a poor man, and I will give you one half of all my fortune if you will . . ."

Marcus laughed, the noise sudden and harsh in the echoing tower. "Mithras! You old men all offer me money. Do you all think I can be bought? You cannot turn the blade of a sword with a small handful of gold."

"My family!"

"My father," mocked Marcus. "You are to die, old man. And all you can do is determine the manner in which you go to meet your death. Isidorus met his badly. Your cousin badly. And I have also slain the seven men involved in the murder of my mother, the Princess Elfleda of the Iceni. None of them died well."

"You! Oh! Your mother and your father both. I

did not know, Marcus Julius Britannicus. I swear upon the graves of my father that I did not know."

"I believe you. But that makes not one speck of difference to what must happen. Come. Up those stairs."

The mill was built in a new manner. The grain was delivered up a ramp on the outside of the tower by a cart, pulled by a mule. It filled up a great vat. Which could be emptied by opening a handle under the roof. That, in turn, allowed the coarse grain to filter slowly through into the actual milling pit. This was a circular structure, an arm's span deep, made out of granite. A huge wheel, hewn from a single block of granite, rolled around this pit, pulled by a pair of mules in a corridor that ran about about the outside of the grinding mill itself.

The flour, a light brown dust, flowed cleanly through a hole at the center of this pit, and passed down a series of funnels and chutes, to the great chamber on the ground floor where it would be collected into sacks.

"It will make us rich," said Vitruvius, as he explained the working of his pet to the man who was standing at his side, waiting to kill him. Marcus saw that the old man had actually forgotten his doom, so keenly did he believe his mill would bring him success.

"And they will think all is ready?"

"Yes. There was no need to tell those men that. My dearest wife knows how it works."

"Show me where the grain is poured in."

"Up here. Take care on the steps. There should be a handrail but those lazy animals have been shirking. Up here."

There was a platform, where two fat mules chewed contentedly on a pile of hay. A system of chains and pulleys raised and lowered an inspection hatch over the pit, so that slaves could crawl into it and clean it out after flour had been ground there. Seeing that the young gladiator was interested in that part of it. Vitruvius lifted it for him, reaching for one of the resin-scented torches from a bracket to show him the interior.

When he went to lower it again, Marcus put out a hand and stopped him.

"Leave it up."

"But my dear young boy . . . what am I doing? You are the man who . . . Your father . . . !"

"Leave it."

An idea had come to Marcus that thrilled him with its simplicity, and the ironic way in which he could destroy this man with his own device. His father had loved a jest with an ironic twist, and Marcus felt sure that this would have pleased him.

It took him only a moment to subdue the noble. Vitruvius was more than twenty years his senior, and had absolutely no chance against the hard, battle-trained gladiator. Marcus was able to bind him, with a strip of cloth cut from the edge of his cloak, using more of the same to gag him, as he had gagged his cousin only an hour or so before.

Then he lowered the body into the pit, panting at the man's weight. Wrinkling his nose at the sour stench of sweat. The sweat of fear. Tucking the remains of Vitruvius's cloak about his white legs, seeing the knots of blue veins that disfigured them.

Suddenly he felt tired. The flame of his anger against the young men who had raped his mother, that had blazed so brightly, had finally burned itself out. For these flabby, aging conspirators with their senile dreams of power, he felt only a sick disgust.

Before he lowered the great stone lid of the grain

bin, he leaned in and looked at the bound man. Vitruvius's eyes met his, and he read the mute plea in them.

"No. I have no speech for you. No honeyed words to roll of my tongue. Just this. My father was a fine and honorable man, and because of your evil he died many years before his time. Now, Metellus Julius Vitruvius, you will finally pay the price for your wickedness. I regret only that this death will be quick."

The chain rattled as he lowered the lid down, the pulleys squeaking and protesting at the strain. Slowly, like a stone being rolled in front of a tomb, total blackness filled the pit. By pressing his ear to the top slab, Marcus could make out the faintest of sounds. Like a mouse scratching behind a thick wall.

And that was all.

He left all things as they were and walked carefully down the stairs to wait in the room on the ground floor for the rest of the guests to attend the opening.

After nearly an hour he realized that Flavia might be waiting for her husband to reappear before setting the others on their way to the mill. So Marcus tucked his cloak about him again and walked across the gardens back to the house, feeling the frost biting into the ground.

Flavia was sober, or more sober than she had been, and was moving with some grace among the guests. Who were becoming rowdy in their eagerness. When she saw Marcus appear in the atrium, she looked away. Then changed her mind and stalked across to him.

"Where is Metellus?"

"I bring a message from him."

"Then give it to me," she snapped. "It is already past the time for beginning the opening."

"Well, my lady." Marcus bowed as low as he could, sweeping his cloak aside. "Your heroic husband, that great defender of the weak and lowly. The fighter against all . . ."

"Get on with it! I don't have all night to listen to you prattle on."

"But he told me most urgently to tell you that he sent you his affection and greetings. To the most divine of wives, whose gleaming honor was not to be measured against rubies or gold. To tell that all was ready."

"At last. And I suppose that you will be coming with us to the mill? Not that I approve of hired killers as house guests, you know."

"But, my lady. Being a killer is all very well, as long as one takes great care who one kills."

Flavia turned away from him, ignoring him, but Marcus still made a deep bow to her retreating back.

At the further doorway she paused as a thought struck her. "Where *is* my husband?"

"The strain and excitement was too much for him. He asked me to make his apologies to all the guests, and asked that you might begin without him. But he said that he would be with you in spirit. I think, my lady, that he was perhaps gone to lie down somewhere. Maybe we shall find out where he has gone once the mill has begun to run."

"And you say all is ready?"

"Yes. Dear Metellus filled the grain bin. All that is needful has been done. It remains only for your serene beauty to pull on the lever which will, as your husband explained it to me, set the mules to moving, and the great stone wheel will begin its grinding."

"And I shall bathe my hands and face in the gentle stream of flour, as I have promised. Very well. You had best gather up the others and we will begin."

A drunk Senator clambered up from the floor, blinking owlishly as he watched the mistress of the house stalk away. "By Jupiter Optimus Maximus! If ever a woman could turn wine to vinegar it is that bitch. I swear there are times that poor Vitruvius believes that he would be better off dead!"

Marcus nodded and laughed. "I would that I could aid him."

But the man was too drunk to appreciate the jest.

There were around twenty or so of the guests that had sobered enough to face the freezing walk across the gardens to the towering bulk of the new mill. The white wood gleamed in the pale moonlight and the air was heavy with the scent of pitch. Flavia, wrapped in a fur-lined gown, with a light green hood, leading the way inside.

"Come on. Come on. It is too bad of Metellus not to come. After all, it was his idea to have this ridiculous party here to grind the first flour."

"It was his dearest wish," said Marcus sententiously from the rear of the crowd. "But he felt the excitement would be just too much for him. He will be with us later."

"Probably laying some slut in the kitchens," whispered a stout man near Marcus. Unfortunately loud enough for Flavia to hear. She turned and chilled him with a glance.

"Well. This is too bad. Really too bad. It would have been so nice."

"What's that?" said someone.

"What?"

"I thought I heard a noise. Something moving."

A silence threatened. Marcus staged a coughing fit, hawking and spluttering. "My apologies, Lady Flavia. I fear that it's the cold reaching my chest. Perhaps the noise was just the building settling in this chill."

"Or mice. Where there's flour, there'll always be mice," said someone else.

"I don't care. But I do intend to begin what we have all come here for."

There was a murmur of agreement, and much rubbing of hands drowning out any noise that there might have been. Marcus recalled a tale that he had been told by his mother, about a Celt who had killed his father. Wrapped the corpse in a hundred layers of cloth. Buried it in a dozen boxes, all nailed down tight. Thrown them into the deepest part of the ocean, weighted with rocks.

And still the man heard, day and night, the noise of his father's heart. Still beating. Until he could stand it no longer and went mad, hanging himself from a grove of willows.

He wondered to himself if Vitruvius had managed to get free and was, even now, struggling with the impossible task of lifting that great lid of stone that entombed him. It was not possible.

Flavia coughed, stilling the noise, drawing attention to herself. "In the lamented absence of my dearest husband, it falls to me to perform this opening, and to make a short speech. We have spent many months on this mill, and hope that all of you will aid us in making it a success. I am sure that we will be prepared to help you in turn with favorable terms for the grinding of your grain. And I am certain that, after you have seen this demonstration tonight, you will agree that you have never seen anything quite like it before."

"Truth! Truth!" called out Marcus, attracting only a venomous glance from the Lady Flavia.

"So I shall now begin. You. You!"

Marcus realized that everyone was looking at him. "What? What, my lady?"

"I said, if you would listen to your betters, gladiator, that I wished to ask you a question."

"Ask away, Lady Flavia. I am ever your most humble and obedient slave."

"Then tell me again what is done."

Patiently, like dealing with a half-wit, Marcus explained it again, with that level of overhumility that it's difficult to pin down as rudeness.

"The grain is where the grain should be. The mules are where they should be. And you are also where you should be. My lady."

"Everyone is where they should be, except old Metellus," laughed someone.

"Perhaps Metellus is also where he should be," whispered Marcus.

But nobody realized the truth of that.

"Then I shall begin. Despite the absence of my dearest husband. I am pleased to pull this lever, which will remove the check on the animals, and they will begin to turn the wheel."

With a straining of muscles, Lady Flavia threw her weight against the lever, and there was a grinding noise from up above. Then silence. For a moment Marcus thought that something must have gone wrong with the mechanism, and strained his ears for a cry.

But the moment passed, and they all felt, rather than heard, the stone wheel begin to grind inexorably around.

He imagined what it must be like up there for Vitruvius. Bound and helpless in that cold darkness, hearing the lever thrown, by his own wife, and the hooves of the mules as they begin to clatter around the track. And that sonorous grating of granite on granite. Getting closer and closer.

And closer.

Her face transfixed with delight at what was happening, Flavia moved under the outlet chute, pushing aside a tall Senator who got in her way. "This will make our fortunes, my lords. I shall keep my promise to my husband, and as the first flood of fine flour gushes forth, I shall stand here, my face upturned, and I shall bathe in it. And you may see it as brown flour. But to me it will be purest gold."

Marcus stood and watched.

Imagining what was happening up above him.

Perhaps Vitruvius had managed to wriggle around ahead of the wheel. Squirming on his belly like a worm before the plough. Straining to try and save himself.

But the stone would be inexorable. Grinding closer and closer.

"Why is nothing coming through?"

"Patience, Lady Flavia. It takes a few moment for the first grain to be crushed."

The first touch on the cringing flesh of the rough, cold stone.

Then the first pain.

Flavia was standing beneath the chute, her eyes closed, like someone experiencing a beatific vision, waiting for the first caress of the flour on her skin. Cascading over her body like a libation from the gods.

Marcus edged nearer to the door of the mill, ready to make his departure.

"I can feel it!" shrieked the lady, ignorant of the stunned and horrified silence around her.

As they watched her bathing in . . . not fine flour, but the stickly crimson lifeblood of her husband.

Marcus was walking away briskly across the quiet gardens before he heard the first scream.

TEN

Despite his health, Marcus contrived to catch a cold that night, and was laid up in bed for three days. Titus had heard the sorry news of the appalling accidents that had befallen the cousins, Vitruvius and Gellius, and had asked his young fighting man to come to the Palace to recover from the illness.

"As a reward for your skill in the arena, you understand, Marcus. You do understand that, don't you? I would not be pleased if I heard that anyone had thought that it might be for anything else."

"I do understand, my Emperor," replied Marcus, raising himself painfully from the bed, feeling a stiffness in every bone. His head aching as though a cascade of drums were pounding in his brain.

Titus sat thoughtfully on the edge of the bed, looking at him. "The word is that the Plague is nearing the city. There are reports coming of it raging through Gaul, and coming ever closer. I have decided, for my health, to take myself and a few friends to a villa I keep in the hills, where we can be free of this pestilence. I would have you come with me."

"The wish of the Emperor is a command, mighty Caesar," grinned Marcus, trying to bow. Now that three of the enemies were dead, the atmosphere was more relaxed. He was more sure than ever that Titus had used his desire for vengeance as his own instrument of state. Eliminating men who might pose a threat to him. But that was no concern of his. He was merely a sharp sword in the hands of the Emperor, and he must slay whoever he was told. But it was good to know that the trail of death was nearly ended.

"They say that Condorus is no better, Marcus. A dozen times he has sent slaves to me, asking when he might be received. And a dozen times they have been sent away with no reply."

"When do you leave, my Emperor?"

"Today. Later, when all is packed."

"I will be on my feet tomorrow. There is one more matter here in Rome that merits my attention. Once that is finally over, might I come to you?"

The Emperor leaned over and embraced him. "I would be pained if you did not. I have grown fond of you, Marcus Julius Britannicus. With me, you shall find advancement. You have my word on it."

"Then we shall meet again, in two days."

It was nearer a week.

Marcus had been weaker than he thought, and when he had attempted to get up, he had again become feverish, and the Imperial physician had refused him permission to move from his room until the humors had quite left him.

When he finally rose and walked from the Palace

into the streets of the Imperial City, he found it like a place of dreams. Everywhere shops and houses were closed and their doors nailed shut with boards.

Ahtough slaves had brought him news of the progress of the sickness through the country, Marcus had not been prepared for the way it had affected people. Here and there men scurried about, faces cloaked against the spread of the disease. Had it not been for the cold, there was little doubt that it would have gained a greater hold.

Carts carried the dead to burial grounds at plague pits beyond the city boundaries. But there were few left to bury. Most had followed the hasty example of their Emperor and taken themselves away to the country. The ones who remained were those who could most easily be spared.

The poor.

The road was quite empty. It was near evening, the pale winter sun vanishing behind the hills, and stars already visible in the dark blue vault.

Marcus wore a cloak of green, over a layer of thick woolen tunic and thick woolen underclothing. Yet the cold still struck through, biting at him. It would be good to go to the hills to relax and let his strength come back to him.

His sword swung at his hip, his studded sandals clacking on the stone of the road as he walked toward his appointment. The house where Vellius Condorus had been living was at the end, set among large gardens. Isolated from the others. The barred iron gates at the front stood open and the small cottage of the gatekeeper was empty. Its door also open, showing every sign of being hastily evacuated.

Letting his hand reach down for the comforting

feel of his sword hilt, Marcus walked slowly up the sweeping drive, finding the front doors were also open. It was very still. The wind rustled the leaves on the trees outside, bringing the last few of them fluttering to the ground. Away to the east he heard the distant rumbling of thunder.

He wondered if he should call, but there was the feeling of desolation. Like an abandoned temple that the elements have taken over. There could be nothing living in that great echoing emptiness. Vellius Condorus must have left Rome during the days that he had been ill.

The thought disturbed him. To be so close and now to begin the hunt again. Though he had little stomach left for the killing, it was not something that could be abandoned.

He pushed inside, his feet disturbing a pile of dry leaves that the wind had carried in. Something moved in the shadows of the corridor ahead of him. He bent and picked up a pebble and shied it at the thing.

It was a rat. A great black creature, so confident in its domain that it hardly hurried away from him, pausing to look over its shoulder with beady eyes, whiskers trembling a little. There were more. As he walked through the empty mansion he heard and saw more. Dozens of them. No doubt feeding on the riches that had been abandoned in the kitchens when the house was left.

It wasn't worth looking in all the rooms. But there was just the chance that Vellius Condorus might have left something behind in his panic. A clue to where he had gone. A document mentioning a plot.

Marcus walked into the master suite of rooms, and recoiled. Gagging at the stench. There was something dead in the rooms. He knew the smell too well to mistake it. A man . . . or a woman . . . had died in there and a corpse now lay rotting in some dark corner. A shutter banged as the wind rose with the gathering storm, making him start, half-drawing his sword. Smiling at his own nerves.

Then a groan.

A human groan!

There was someone alive in that charnel-house. Cautiously Marcus eased open the door to the sleeping rooms, and saw a great rumpled bed, its linen stained with old blood, and soaked with excrement.

On the bed lay . . .

"Vellius Condorus. Hail!"

Marcus walked across the room and threw open the shutters, so that the last beams of the setting sun flooded in and illuminated the figure on the bed. And when he saw his last enemy, Marcus turned away.

He had seen lepers about, they were a common enough sight. Their leonine faces, and stumps of fingers, insensate to pain. Rotting sockets at the center of their faces, fringed with shreds of dead flesh, where their noses had once been.

But they were nothing compared to this.

At first he doubted the man could still be alive, but the mouth moved, and the faintest of sounds came from the cracked and swollen lips.

Marcus stood back, wanting to leave, and yet strangely compelled to draw nearer. Not to gloat over the man, though he had reason enough. He had to force himself to remember that this man had helped plot the death of his father. And had been one of the gang who had held down his mother and spent their lust between her thighs. And then tortured and killed her. This man. This Vellius Condorus.

His body was naked, the sheets crumpled and torn where he had tossed and raved in the grip of an awful fever. Marcus had heard enough of the symptoms from the Imperial physician to know what Condorus had been through.

A sickness that began with a cold and weakness. Aching in the head and back that racked the sufferer, bringing on fits of vomiting that weakened still further. The bowels opened uncontrollably, and the body became pale.

Condorus's face had changed almost beyond recognition from the red-cheeked heavy features of the official that Marcus had first met back in Britannia. Now there was not a grain of spare flesh on that white face. There was a thread of dark brown across the mouth and jaw where Condorus had suffered a nosebleed that was such a common feature of this plague.

And there were the swellings.

Great black boils that festered on his body. Swelling in his groin, and in his neck, and under the arms. Those in the groin the size of a lemon. Those under the arms the size of a pigeon's egg. Some had burst, and dried matter was crusted across the ribs, prominent as the noble fought for every breath.

Marcus knew that there was nothing that he could do for the man. Condorus was as doomed as if he had thrust a sword into his heart.

"So. It is over at last."

Marcus's words disturbed the man on the bed. And also sent the waiting rats into the deepest shadows. There seemed to be more of them than before.

"Who . . . ?"

"Marcus Julius Britannicus."

"You are too late, my friend. Your work has been done for you."

A spasm shook Condorus and he tried to scream with the pain, but his mouth was dry, lips skinning, and all that came was a strangled croaking noise.

"Am I the last?"

"Yes."

"All . . . all dead?"

"All dead."

Condorus lay back again, resembling the corpse that he would soon become. Marcus had half unsheathed his sword, intending to end it. But it was pointless. The man was not worth soiling his blade for. Silently, he turned to leave, when the dying man spoke again.

"Kill me."

"No. No, Condorus. There is too much between us for that mercy."

"I beg you."

"No." Marcus laughed quietly. "Every one of the others. There have been a dozen, Condorus. Near every one begged me. But they begged me for life. They offered me all things. Gold. Power. For life. And now you, the last and the worst of my enemies, beg for death. No."

Condorus panted for breath, watching as Marcus walked away from the room, passing through the dusty beam of sunlight near the door.

"Wait. The dark. Light me a torch, Marcus Julius Britannicus, that I may go in the darkness. And it will keep back the rats."

Marcus had gone.

It took him several minutes to find and light a torch. By the time he brought it back, sending the rats cheeping and scampering from the bed, Vellius Condorus was dead.

He left the torch burning brightly in a sconce at

the corner of the room, over the bed, tugging a sheet across the distorted face of the corpse.

And walked from the house, into the cool of the winter evening.

ELEVEN

It was scorchingly hot, the scent of death and blood hanging heavy over the greasy water.

The cries for Vulpus fading away like the dew on a summer morning as the vast crocodile lurched from the water, its claws furrowing the mud as it scrambled toward Marcus. Its tail thrashed at the pool, sending up scummy ripples that rocked the tangle of bodies floating together near the island.

The creature was vast. Quite the biggest river worm that Marcus had ever seen. The bestiarius must be doing well from this Games. Its silver collar glittered in the sun as it stopped a few paces from him, its yellow eyes unflickering as it watched him.

Without the least warning . . . it charged!

In the cool corridor at the rear of the Colosseum, Helvius Geminus heard the roar of the crowd and knew that the climax of the day was at hand. And he fretted impatiently, torn between the desire to see Vulpus fight the lizard, and the desire to conform to the right standards and remain with his wife as the physician forced his fingers down her throat to pluck out the wedge of honeyed dates that were choking her.

Propriety won.

He stayed with Poppaea.

"Mithras!"

The God of the Legions must have heard the cry, for Marcus was able to dodge that first, cripplingly quick attack, half-jumping and half-slipping down the far side of the island, mud and blood streaking his arms and legs, looking up the slope to where the leviathan now dominated the battle from the higher ground.

The next time it came at him, his back would be to the water. The natural element of the beast.

When the second attack came, the crocodile moved more slowly, its scaly tail swishing from side to side, barring Marcus from getting past it. Forcing him back toward the water. Back.

The mob stayed surprisingly silent after the first roar, watching their hero preparing for the battle.

"There!" The physician threw a handful of squashed dates on the stone floor, coated with spittle.

Geminus looked down at his wife who was at last breathing normally, her mouth sagging wide open. Tears streaking down her cheeks at the relief.

"Will she be all right now?"

"Aye. I warrant that her throat and mouth will be paining her for a few days. Probably stop her talking for a while."

Geminus would have smiled but Poppaea was watching him.

"Keep her quiet. That's all."

What was going on out there? Helvius Geminus bent down by the side of his wife, stroking away an errant ringlet of hair from her forehead.

The warm wetness touched his feet, and Marcus knew there was nowhere else to run to. The crocodile seemed to know it as well, opening its great jaws, showing the rows of savage teeth. The miasma of rotting meat and fish enveloped Marcus.

A hiss of breath, and the creature was on him, snapping at his legs as it came. The crowd yelled as they watched Volpus live up to his reputation for never doing the obvious. Where most men would have tried to escape, and been dragged under and killed, or made a useless slash with their swords at the armored hide, Marcus leaped *forward*, on top of it!

Some years back he had passed time in the company of an aged bestiarius, and they had talked long into the night about animals. Their habits. Their strengths.

Their weaknesses.

And they had talked of the river worm of the east. The way it attacked and rolled, breaking and crushing and drowning. Its plated skin. Its teeth.

Its weakness.

"Once those jaws close on you, then you can bid a farewell to the world, for no power can open them. Yet the Gods give you a chance. For once those jaws are held *closed*, even a maid could keep them so. The beast has no power to force them open."

Clutching his sword in the right hand, Marcus crashed down on top of the beast, his arms clamping around the gaping jaws, tugging on them. Squeezing.

Forcing them closed. The tail thrashed furiously, sending up a blinding curtain of mud and sand. But Marcus held on.

"Stop it from getting into the water. It'll dive under and you have to let go or drown. If you let go it'll turn on an aureus and have you."

Marcus hadn't forgotten that part of the advice, either.

While it tried to move him, he struggled to shorten his sword to stab at its eye, but it was too strong, nearly throwing him off. It even rolled, but he braced his legs into the blood-soaked mud and stopped it, straining with all power. Knowing that its weight could crush and cripple him.

When that failed, it made its bid for the lake.

"How is . . . is Vulpus?" croaked Poppaea, as she tried to get to her feet.

An old gladiator, his face seamed with a scar that tugged down his eye and slashed his nose in two unequal parts, acting as an attendant, had been hovering around helpfully, hoping for a small reward for his efforts. He raised his knuckles to his forehead.

"I'll go and look, my lady. And come back immediately to tell you."

It meant taking a desperate chance, but there was no other choice. Marcus had to partly let go his hold on the jaws, risking being mauled.

But by doing that he was able to use his right hand. And his gladius. Swinging it up and back, while the crowd roared their approval of his tactics. Lunging for the hooded eye. Stabbing hard. Again and again.

Feeling the blade jarring against the bony skin of the crocodile. The jaws straining against his left arm, slowly, but surely, opening, ready to savage him.

Striking again and again, in furious desperation. Until he succeeded. Feeling the sword slide home with no resistance at all, slicing through the eye. Making the reptile buck and hiss in pain.

Hitting for the other eye. This time, knowing where to strike, blinding it, so that it thrashed and kicked, showering him in mud, clear liquid spurting from its eyes.

Finally throwing him off on his side. Marcus rolled to his feet while the screams from the crowd reached a deafening hysteria. The beast scenting the water, and trying to lumber toward it. Pausing as he hit it a ringing blow on the side of the head, making it stop, lifting up its blind eyes, exposing the soft white folds of skin under its throat.

"Vulpus! Vulpus!"

Lunging at the spot, feeling the blade ease through the skin, the blood jetting out over his hands. Withdrawing and thrusting again. The crocodile drawing itself up, and clawing at the air, then rolling on its back, legs kicking. Blood coming from its mouth.

Marcus dodging the legs and the snapping jaws to plunge his gladius one more time into its belly, ripping it open, so that its guts spilled out in the mud and it quivered and so died.

"The crowd are going made, my lady," reported the old man, his legs trembling from the excitement that crackled in the warm air of the Colosseum.

"And he lives? Marcus, my dearest hero, he still lives?"

"Aye."

"The Gods be praised." Poppaea began to cry, great tears of relief falling across her reddened cheeks, while all about her the cries and cheers swelled, filling the summer day.

"Aye," said the old gladiator. "Vulpus lives to fight again. And again. And again."

THE INCREDIBLE ACTION PACKED SERIES

DEATH MERCHANT

by Joseph Rosenberger

His name is Richard Camellion, he's a master of disguise, deception and destruction. He does what the CIA and FBI cannot do.

Order		Title	Book #	Price
_____	# 1	THE DEATH MERCHANT	P211	$ .95
_____	# 2	OPERATION OVERKILL	P245	$ .95
_____	# 3	THE PSYCHOTRON PLOT	P117	$ .95
_____	# 4	CHINESE CONSPIRACY	P168	$ .95
_____	# 5	SATAN STRIKE	P182	$ .95
_____	# 6	ALBANIAN CONNECTION	P670	$1.25
_____	# 7	CASTRO FILE	P264	$ .95
_____	# 8	BILLIONAIRE MISSION	P339	$ .95
_____	# 9	THE LASER WAR	P399	$ .95
_____	#10	THE MAINLINE PLOT	P473	$1.25
_____	#11	MANHATTAN WIPEOUT	P561	$1.25
_____	#12	THE KGB FRAME	P642	$1.25
_____	#13	THE MATO GROSSO HORROR	P705	$1.25
_____	#14	VENGEANCE OF THE GOLDEN HAWK	P796	$1.25
_____	#15	THE IRON SWASTIKA PLOT	P823	$1.25
_____	#16	INVASION OF THE CLONES	P857	$1.25
_____	#17	THE ZEMLYA EXPEDITION	P880	$1.25

TO ORDER

Please check the space next to the book/s you want, send this order form together with your check or money order, include the price of the book/s and 25¢ for handling and mailing to:
PINNACLE BOOKS, INC. / P.O. Box 4347
Grand Central Station / New York, N.Y. 10017

☐ CHECK HERE IF YOU WANT A FREE CATALOG

I have enclosed $_____ check_____ or money order_____ as payment in full. No C.O.D.'s.

Name_____

Address_____

City_____ State_____ Zip_____
(Please allow time for delivery.)   PB-36

3061

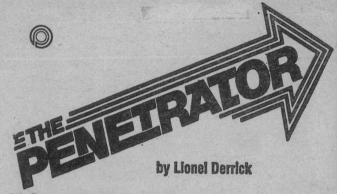

THE PENETRATOR

by Lionel Derrick

Mark Hardin. Discharged from the army, after service in
Vietnam. His military career was over. But *his* war was
just beginning. His reason for living and reason for dying
became the same—to stamp out crime and corruption
wherever he finds it. He is deadly; he is unpredictable;
and he is dedicated. He is The Penetrator!

Read all of him in:

Order			Title	Book No.	Price
————	#	1	THE TARGET IS H	P236	$ .95
————	#	2	BLOOD ON THE STRIP	P237	$ .95
————	#	3	CAPITOL HELL	P318	$ .95
————	#	4	HIJACKING MANHATTAN	P338	$ .95
————	#	5	MARDI GRAS MASSACRE	P378	$ .95
————	#	6	TOKYO PURPLE	P434	$1.25
————	#	7	BAJA BANDIDOS	P502	$1.25
————	#	8	THE NORTHWEST CONTRACT	P540	$1.25
————	#	9	DODGE CITY BOMBERS	P627	$1.25
————	#	10	THE HELLBOMB FLIGHT	P690	$1.25

NORTH COMPLEX